MURDER WORLD
KAIJU DAWN

JASON CORDOVA & ERIC S BROWN

INTERLUDE I

"Please state your name for the record."

The man fumbled with the microphone for a moment before he spoke, his tone filled with nerves and fear. In the small, cramped room, there was barely enough space for him, the prosecutor who sat across from him, and the four armed Marines. The air was hot and humid. Between the armed guards and the way they continued to finger the triggers of their rifles, he was almost certain that he would not be walking out of the interrogation room alive.

"James Ambrose."

"And what is your occupation, Mister Ambrose?"

"I'm the owner of Intergalactic Shipping and Freight, which consists of twelve for-hire merchant vessels. This includes the merchant vessel Fancy."

"But you are not its captain?"

"No sir," the pudgy businessman said as he wiped sweat from his brow. "I lease her out to other individuals on yearly contracts."

"And to whom is the vessel Fancy currently leased?"

"Ah, that would be Captain Vincente Huerta, sir."

"And have you had any contact with Captain Huerta in the past six months?"

"No," Ambrose said as he continued to sweat profusely under the withering gaze of the Prosecutor. "He still has lease on the ship for another two months, and since he's leased out the ship for five years now, he usually just deposits the money he owes into my account."

"You do realize that in a Court of Law, your business transactions come under the scrutiny of the Tax Revenue Service, and that all your transactions regarding Captain Huerta and the Fancy will be audited?"

"I do, sir."

"Very well," the Prosecutor flipped through his screen for a moment before he paused and looked back up at the man. "Mister

Ambrose, what can you tell us about Captain Huerta? Something that wouldn't be on financial records? Something that only his associates would know?"

James Ambrose thought for a moment before he answered, "Well, I can tell you one thing for certain, sir."

"And that is?"

"He's a goddamned lunatic, uh, sir."

CHAPTER ONE

"Vincente!" A woman's voice jarred him awake. He cracked open his eyes, rubbed away the filth and grime, and struggled to sit up in his bunk. He fumbled around for a moment as he searched for his comm unit. His hand smacked against the metal frame of his bunk and he yelped in pain. He blinked twice as he realized that he was on the floor, his bed was above him, and an empty bottle of booze was under his back.

For a moment, he wondered just how he had ended up there, until memories of the night before came back to him. He groaned and put his head back down on the cool floor, ignoring the bottle pressing into his sciatica. He'd slept on worse things in the past, though nothing so bad recently.

His gung-ho days of yore were long behind him.

"Way too much whiskey," he muttered. "Can't drink a fifth anymore without paying the price. Ugh. What was I thinking? Lights on."

The overhead light of his room turned on, casting a harsh glare about. Vincente winced as his head began to throb. He pulled himself up off the floor and stumbled over to the small, steel mirror above his sink. Spitting in the sink, Vincente tried to clear his mouth of the foul taste. He glanced at himself and was appalled at who was looking back at him.

Unshaven cheeks with unkempt hair, he looked every part the scoundrel his first ex-wife's family had called him from the moment they laid eyes on him long before. His eyes were bloodshot, and he felt an unpleasant and familiar fuzz over his teeth. He exhaled and gagged as the overwhelming stench of cheap booze hit him again.

"Jesus..." Vincente hissed, holding back the urge to vomit. If his breath was that bad, he was almost afraid of how much worse his clothes were.

"Vincente!"

"What?!" he roared back and winced as a fresh jolt of pain tore through him. "Ow. Shit, my head..."

"Comm call," the reply came. "I think it's for a job."

"Damn it," he muttered as his blue eyes inspected the rest of him in the mirror. "I look like shit. Can you stall?"

"I've been stalling for fifteen minutes, you fat old drunk!"

"Right," he breathed. "Okay, be there in a minute. Get me a stim, will you?"

"I'm not your servant!"

"I'm still your boss. Stimulant. Now."

"Old, fat bastard..." the voice trailed off as his pilot moved down the corridor.

He turned on the faucet and splashed a little water on his face. The cold shocked him awake, though it also made the sledgehammer pounding at his temples more evident. He toweled his face dry and turned off the water.

"I still look like hell," he said before shrugging. "Screw it."

He stumbled over to his hatch and popped it open. The oil-and-recycled oxygen smell nearly overwhelmed him as the new scents collided with the booze-soaked atmosphere of his room. He shook his head, struggling to regain his bearings. He glanced towards the cockpit, where his pilot was returning with a stim in her hand. He smiled as he saw the small medical device.

"Thanks, Jasmine."

"Thank me later," she said as she handed him the small injector. "When you're in immense pain after this wears off and I'm mocking you. I'll feel better about it then. I might even gloat some about how I'm always right and you're always stupid." He pressed it against his neck pulled the trigger. Immediately, the neural stimulators went to work, temporarily ridding him of any and all symptoms of his hangover. He sighed with great pleasure as the hangover disappeared and his brain was not as mushy as it had been.

"Ah, bliss," he murmured. "Blessed light, this is good stuff for a hangover. So, what do we know about the potential client?"

"Sounds desperate," Jasmine said as she flipped her long, braided hair over one shoulder. "Nice clothes, good haircut. Has had some minor cosmetic nanosurgery on his face to make him look slightly different, but nothing major, so he's done some covert work or cheated on his wife recently with a younger woman. My guess is he's either a spook or military."

"Military, huh? Interesting," Vincente said as he made his way to the cockpit. Once there, he plopped down into his seat and looked over at the comm. It was blinking yellow. He shot a questioning glance at Jasmine, who shook her head.

"They tried to lock our comms down when they came calling," she explained. "I had to bypass the main sequencers just so they'd think they had locked us out. I think they didn't want to leave any evidence of them calling. I've already made triplicates, and I'm recording it as well, just in case."

"So they don't know about the upgrades?"

"If they did, they'd have already hung up on us. No, we're good."

"Good girl," he said. He took a deep breath and exhaled slowly. "Okay, I think I'm ready."

"You look horrible, boss."

"Can't be helped," he stated. "Let's see who's calling today, shall we?"

He activated his comm and the light turned green. Four seconds later, a face appeared on the screen. Vincente nodded. Jasmine had been correct about the potential client, as usual. He knew that there had been a reason he continued to tolerate her insolence.

"This is Captain Vincente Huerta of the Fancy. How can I help you today?"

"I'm looking for the individual who once transported fifty tons of uncut diamonds for the Mossdale Cartel from right under the noses of the Morathi State Security," the man on the comm said. "Did I find the right person?"

"That's somewhat private information you have there, mister," Vincente said as he stared at the comm. Only seven people alive knew about that haul, and two of them were on his ship at that moment. Very shortly, he was going to have a talk with someone about how to keep secrets. If he ever did figure out precisely who that person was. "And you are?"

"You may call me Hines."

"No rank, Mister Military Man?"

"Just... Hines."

"So mysterious," Vincente grunted. "Fine, have it your way. So how can I be of service to you?"

"We need you to retrieve vital, sensitive information from a research vessel which has crash-landed on a planet near a quarantine zone," Hines said through the comm. The delay was down to a miniscule four seconds now, and Vincente was pleased with the comm unit upgrade he had purchased on the black market two months before. Granted, if Hines ever figured out that the Fancy had military grade hardware, Vincente would be looking at a few years in a labor camp. "The planet is coded as Gorgon IV, and we'll pay you well for your troubles."

"So send in the Marines," Vincente said, his voice hoarse. He rubbed his face and tried to keep the smile off his face as credit signs bounced around in his head. Off to the side, he saw Jasmine make a face at him. He sighed. The woman just would not let his appearance be, apparently.

"It's outside controlled space," Hines replied.

"And Marines only go to fun, vacation resorts and never have to break things?"

"We have our reasons," Hines said. Vincente finally grinned.

"You bastards were out in Zebulun space again, 'researching', and you lost a spy ship– I'm sorry, a 'research vessel'– and you can't send in any sanctioned rescue involving military personnel, even black ops, because then, someone will know just how badly you fucked up, and you like your rank and pay, and really dislike failure. Am I right? Tell me I'm right. I know I'm right."

"Will you take the job or not?" Hines growled, his pitch low and dangerous.

"Half a mil up front, five million upon delivery of the data banks of your," he made quotations motions in the air with his fingers, "research vessel," Vincente said.

"What?!"

"That's strange. I didn't stutter, and I know I didn't speak in a language you're unfamiliar with."

"You're out of your goddamned mind! I should just shoot you for cause and hire someone else!"

"You already tried that," Vincente said, his grin widening. "Trying to hire someone else, I mean. They all told you to blow off. You only came to me as a last resort, which means I get to dictate the price. Sucks, don't it?"

"I don't have to take this–"

"Yes, you do," Vicente said. "Keep arguing and the price doubles."

"Fine! Half a million credits, wired into your personal account..."

"I have a numbered account available that I would prefer to use," Vincente interrupted again as he began to type on the keyboard. He sent the information to Hines. "It's on Kaymin."

"That's tax dodging!" Hines roared, his face beginning to turn red.

"That's inadmissible in court," Vincente said calmly. "Comm relays are unreliable and can be faked or corrupted. Besides, it's not tax dodging at all. It's simply the military transferring funds to an unknown entity in neutral space. You can't tell me that it's never been done before, Hines. The direct transfer avoids any... problems we might have Tax Revenue Service. I don't want to break the law. I'm a law-abiding citizen, and tax dodging is a crime."

"The hell you are. Fine, you'll have your money within the hour."

"Excellent," Vincente leaned back in his chair and smiled. "It's a pleasure doing business with you, Hines."

"Fuck off, you pirate." the comm call ended. Vincente swiveled his chair around and found Jasmine staring at him. He shrugged his shoulders and abstractedly waved a hand in the direction of the comm.

"Think I asked for too much?"

"Too little," she grunted. His eyes widened in surprise. "Do you know what people in that sector call Gorgon IV?"

"No... and I have a feeling I should," Vincente admitted.

"You ever heard of Murder World?"

"Yeah, sure, everyone's heard of– wait. Seriously? That place is real?"

"As real as you or I," Jasmine said.

"Shit."

"That's what you get for getting so damned drunk last night. I thought you were just crazy to accept the job, not stupid and ignorant."

"I can always say I changed my mind," he muttered as he turned back around. "Just gotta get on the comm..."

"Too late," Jasmine said and passed over the small banking tablet. She jabbed a finger at the account balance, which was now markedly higher than it had before the comm call. "Money's already been deposited. We have to do it."

"Damn it. Now what?"

"Now we go to Murder World," Jasmine said, "and probably die. Momma said that following you around would kill me one day. I just thought it'd be much later than this. Thanks a lot, by the way."

"We're going to need a crew," Vincente moaned as he rested his elbows on the console. He buried his face in his hands. "Besides you and Kamol, I mean. Probably have to pay them well, too. Bunch of damned mercenaries. You know how much money it costs to get a mercenary squad together? Then we have to buy their armor, ammo, food..."

"Psychopaths," Jasmine added, her lips pursed in a thoughtful manner. "That's the only type of people we're going to be able to hire. We try to hire non-crazies and they'll chicken out the minute they hear that we're headed for Murder World. And there's only one place in this sector that has the kind of psychotic scumbags needed..."

"Alawi," Vincente sighed. "I'm going to have to go back to Alawi and see–"

"And apologize to her."

"–and apologize to that, that–"

"Lady?"

"–contemptible, soulless bitch–"

"She's going to shoot you again if you talk like that. I may have to help her."

"–and she's going to want a cut of the money as well–"

"Well, you did cheat her out of over one hundred thousand credits."

"–just to let me even begin to try and hire someone sitting inside her bar willing to sign on and go die with us," Vincente finished. He glared at Jasmine, who smiled serenely at him. He looked at her with a quizzical expression. "You, you really think Mooney's going to shoot me again?"

"Definitely," Jasmine nodded. "She might even aim for something vital this time, like your di–"

"I hate that woman," Vincente said as he rubbed his temples. "Damn. The stim is wearing off. Can I have another?"

"Tough," Jasmine said as she walked out of the cabin. "One every twelve hours. Sorry. Serves you right, though."

"Women," Vincente muttered as the first wave of his monstrous hangover crashed over him.

CHAPTER TWO

"Fancy, you are cleared to land at docking bay fourteen. Please be prepared to declare any fruits or live animals upon arrival," the voice squawked over the comm.

"Thank you, Control. Fancy, out," Jasmine killed the comm and looked back over her shoulder. "Relax, boss. If she'd really wanted you dead, she'd have hired someone to finish the job years ago."

"Or else she wants to do it herself," Vincente mumbled as Jasmine guided the Fancy into a controlled descent through the thick atmosphere of the small moon.

Ever since he had realized that he would have to go to Alawi to recruit his mercenaries, Vincente had been a nervous wreck. He paced the corridors tirelessly as he thought of every single way that Mooney Starchild Glow could murder him, and each new way was worse than the previous one.

"Traffic Control has us on auto now and is taking us in," Jasmine said as she popped out of the cockpit. She watched Vincente pace nervously up and down the hall for a moment before she interrupted his private musings. "You should probably put some body armor on. Just in case, you know, she doesn't wait for you to explain."

"I don't know where it is," Vincente muttered as his pace increased. "Hell, I don't even know if it fits anymore."

Jasmine shook her head. "Just apologize, offer to pay her back, and she'll forgive you. Probably."

Vincente snorted. "Pigs'll fly. How long until we're on the ground?"

"About eight minutes," Jasmine said after casting a quick look at the display terminal. "We're fourth in their queue, but there's a tramp freighter ahead of us. Big old Tibetan."

"Ugh," Vincente groaned. "Those things should be banned."

"I'm going to grab a few things," she said. "You should probably let Kamol know what's going on."

"Right," he breathed as Jasmine disappeared down the long corridor. He activated the ship's internal comms and buzzed the engineer. "Kamol? You alive down there?"

"Ravki lunga dou?"

"No, you're not supposed to be dead," Vincente sighed. Some aliens understood human mannerisms and slang, but the Lorn was not one of them. On the plus side, they were fantastic engineers, and some of the most sought-after crew in all of known space. "We're going to try to hire some folks for a job. Watch the ship, and don't let any customs agent on board."

"Shishika dou?"

"The hell if I know," Vincente admitted. "Kick their ass? Just don't kill them, even if they force the issue. We can always claim you thought they were trying to steal the ship, and you don't understand all human languages."

"Forthraki cona din louda."

"I know you understand them all, but they won't," Vincente reminded the alien. "Okay, just keep it locked up until we come back. Shouldn't be more than a couple of hours."

"Sazhu."

Vincente released the comm button and looked over at Jasmine, who had already put her battle armor on beneath the designer blouse. She tucked a miniscule pistol into the small of her back, where a cleverly disguised holster lay. She grabbed two stun grenades and slipped the square explosives into pouches in her pants. She glanced at him and shrugged.

"Always be prepared."

He shook his head. "I'm glad you are. I don't think anything can prepare me for what's going to happen next."

"Gee, boss, it's almost like you're expecting a fight."

"Oh, I know a fight's going to happen," he admitted. "I'm just hoping it doesn't escalate."

"I promise to behave," Jasmine said, "until someone pulls out a knife. Then I start killing people."

"Can't ask for anything more than that," he allowed.

****

The duo stopped just outside the entrance to the brightly lit bar.

"I can't do this," Vincente muttered. His eyes looked up and down the exterior of the building, drinking in the gaudy decor and twinkling neon lights. Pink storm shutters adorned the garishly green-painted walls, while two bright spotlights atop the roof shone constantly into the dark, cloudy sky, creating the illusion of a full moon. Horrid music emanated from within, a cacophony of noise and drums, which Vincente was able to identify as an interesting clash of blues and industrial styles of music. "We can hire someone else, right? Someone who doesn't want to put a bullet in me. Or has already? Hell, we can do it ourselves, can't we?"

"You have to do this," Jasmine reminded him. "I'm good, but we need meat shields. Big slabs of meat able to soak up a lot of gunfire for me. And you, lard butt. So get your besotted derrière inside and prepare to face the music."

"I'm still your boss," Vincente sighed, "damn it."

He stepped forward and pushed through the windscreen, the small shield allowing them to enter while blocking out the outside elements and any small insects. Jasmine followed closely behind, staying slightly to his left, using her boss as cover while ensuring that she was able to watch his back at the same time. They both knew that there were people inside who would gladly see him dead.

The bar was lively and loud, with an actual live band crooning the latest hit from a small stage in the corner. The main room of the bar was thick with smoke, and the retro lighting in the place made him feel as though he had stepped two thousand years into the past. The bar top was laminate glass, nearly indestructible, and there was more than enough space for Vincente and Jasmine to sidle up to the bar and order drinks.

"Two fingers worth of scotch, neat," he ordered. The bartender, a small, cute young woman who vaguely reminded Vincente of a vid star he had seen once, nodded and poured him a drink. He glanced over at Jasmine. "You getting anything?"

"Nope," she said as she glanced around the bar. "One of us needs to keep their head together."

"Hey! Liquid courage," he said and slipped his cred card to the bartender. He leaned across the bar. "Get me a small tab running, will you? Stop it at thirty, please."

"Thirty, got it," she nodded and took the card. She slipped it underneath the counter in front of him. "You look kinda familiar. Do I know you?"

"Doubtful," Vincente said. The woman had not been working at the bar the last time he had set foot in the place, but he could be wrong. Better not to take any chances. "Can you do me a favor?"

"I'm not a working girl," she said. He shook his head.

"No, I'm not looking for that," he explained. "Is Mooney here?"

"Ms. Mooney? She's always here, mister."

"Yeah, well," Vincente cleared his throat, suddenly feeling very awkward. "Can you tell her that... a friend is here?"

"She's got a lot of friends, mister," the bartender's eyes narrowed. "Which one should I say is calling?"

He took a deep breath. "Tell her Vincente is here."

The bartender's eyes went round. "Oh!"

The bar, which had been jovial and loud upon their entrance, was now quiet. He felt the atmosphere shift, and suddenly a burning desire to leave came over him. He glanced down at Jasmine, who was tense and nervous as well. There were times few and far between in which the diminutive pilot was worried in a place like this, and during those times, Vincente paid more attention to his surroundings.

Fortunately for them, their would-be attackers were less than subtle.

"Vincente Huerta," a particularly vile looking fellow said as he backed away from the virtual gaming console, which was propped up against one of the walls. He turned and sauntered over to where Vincente and Jasmine stood. Behind him followed two larger men. He sneered as he drew closer. "I thought I smelled something foul."

"Naw, that's just that hair lip of yours," Vincente offered helpfully. Ignoring the ugly look that flashed across the man's face, he continued. "You should get that waxed. I bet shaving is a bitch."

"That ain't funny, fat man."

"Hey, you smelled something, and I was offering suggestions," Vincente shrugged. He offered the man a smile. "Do I know you? You'd think I'd remember such an ugly mug, but age and alcohol have a funny way of messing up one's memories."

"Captain..." Jasmine warned in a low voice.

The leader of the trio looked at Jasmine and smirked. "Nice tits."

"Nice face," she retorted, her face turning slightly red. People who did not know better might have assumed she was blushing. Vincente, though, had been around her long enough to recognize that reaction. She was annoyed, which was one step from angry. Vincente internally sighed. "Hate for something bad to happen to it," she finished.

"What's that supposed to mean?"

Vincente put all his weight into the haymaker and let loose, his clenched fist connecting solidly with the man's eye. Something popped in his knuckle as he hit him, but Vincente was more than satisfied with the result as the other man stumbled back. A swift kick to his stomach and Vincente made sure that he was out of the fight.

Unfortunately, that left his two larger friends still standing and very angry.

Vincente grabbed a beer bottle from the bar top and slammed it against the temple of one of the men, who grunted but managed to stay upright. The bottle did not break, which caused Vincente to curse as reverberations from the impact numbed his hand slightly.

"I hate these new laminate bottles!" he yelled as he was picked up by the second man and tossed on a table. He landed heavily, slid off the top and landed on two different men's laps. All three of them tumbled over and landed heavily on the floor.

Vincente picked himself up off the two men and dusted off his shirt. "Thanks for breaking my fall."

"Asshole!" one of them yelled, and promptly punched the man lying next to him in the mouth. He jerked a card out from his opponent's sleeve. "You been cheating!"

"Oh, for the love of..." Vincente muttered and all hell broke loose within the bar.

"Damn it, Vincente!" Jasmine screamed as her hand flashed out and caught the unprotected throat of a drunk who had stumbled too close. He gagged as her strong hand drove into his larynx, nearly crushing the delicate bone. He stumbled to the ground, out of the fight. She drove her knee into the stomach of another man, and for good measure, smashed her elbow across his face, breaking his nose. She kicked him in the groin and let him fall to the floor. "Every. Goddamned. Time!"

"I'm sorry!" Vincente called back as he slammed another beer bottle over the head of one of his attackers. This one broke, albeit reluctantly, but that was good enough for him. The man dropped like a felled ox. "I thought I was being polite!"

Jasmine did not answer as she vaulted onto a table and kicked another full bottle of beer into the face of a man who was about the attack her captain from behind. He yowled loudly as the bottle broke his teeth and cut his lips. She dropped almost flat on her back as a knife swept through the air where her neck had been moments before and grabbed her new attacker by the belt. She used her momentum to bring her legs up and she quickly wrapped them around his neck. She twisted her thighs and felt a satisfying crunch as his neck broke. He fell and Jasmine landed on top of him, his large frame cushioning her fall. She rolled off to the side and narrowly dodged another beer bottle.

"No knives!" she shouted and punched someone new in the face. Teeth flew. "A brawl doesn't need knives!"

"Chairs are okay," Vincente added and swung the chair in his hands, breaking it on the back of a particularly large man. The man stood still for a moment before rising to his full height. He swiveled and looked at Vincente with his one good eye. Vincente groaned. "Sonofa—"

The giant grabbed Vincente by the throat and tossed him across the bar, sending him through two tables and four men. Vincente landed heavily on the floor but managed to stagger back to his feet, his head swimming. He looked around and raised his fists, but nobody else moved closer.

"C'mon, I'm just getting warmed up," he said, staggering forward."

The fight ended as quickly as it began as a tall, thin figure walked out from the back room. Vincente's eyes widened as he recognized the woman, and the weapon that she held in her hands.

"Hello, darling," a soft voice whispered before him as the barrel of a shotgun gleamed in the light of the room. "Never thought I'd see you around these parts again."

CHAPTER THREE

The bar was deathly quiet. Vincente peered through the smoke and haze and faintly recognized the owner of the bar standing in front of him. He wasn't too certain, though. The last hit to the head had shaken some cobwebs loose.

"Give me one good reason why I shouldn't blow your head off right now," Mooney growled as she leveled the shotgun at him. Vincente raised his hands slowly into the air.

He hadn't been mistaken. It was a shame, really. He had been looking forward to living a long life.

"You won't ever get paid," Jasmine squeaked from behind him. Mooney made a jerking motion with the shotgun.

"Get out from back there, girl," Mooney said. "I don't want you to get blood on that pretty blouse."

"Thanks," Jasmine said and slid out of the line of fire. "It's a Don Capistrano."

"Oh, nice," Mooney's eyes went back to the blouse. "Where'd you get it from?"

"Ezekiel Station just got a bunch in before we took our most recent job," Jasmine said as she tugged the fabric a little. "Breathes well for when you're on a ship, and is pretty good at repelling smells."

"Set you back some?"

"I know a guy, so it wasn't that bad," Jasmine explained.

"You and I should talk business some time. You seem to have connections everywhere."

"I'm a popular girl, what can I say?"

"Excuse me?" Vincente waved a hand. "Can I say something?"

"No," both women replied at once.

"He's got the money to pay you back," Jasmine said, once she was certain that Mooney wasn't going to shoot her.

"He does, does he?" Mooney looked over at Vincente, who offered her a rakish smile. She scoffed. "Don't even try it. It looked good fifty pounds and fifteen years ago. Now it just looks like you have indigestion and an ulcer."

"Hey!"

"He can pay half now, and the rest of what he owes you when he gets back from the job he was hired to do," Jasmine offered.

"People are dumb enough to hire this old drunk?"

"Desperate enough, yeah."

"Oh, come on!" Vincente practically howled.

"Fine," Mooney sniffed and lowered the shotgun. "I want the hundred thousand you owe me now, and five percent of whatever you're being paid."

"Are you out of your damned mind?"

"Ten percent."

"Okay, okay, I'm sorry, five percent," Vincente did some mental math in his head. "That'll make you...fifty thousand credits wealthier."

"Bullshit," Mooney laughed at him, "you're a crook. You charged more than one million."

"You're ruthless," Vincente said. "Seventy-five thousand credits. That's five percent of what I got."

"You lying to me?" Mooney waggled the shotgun. "I can always toughen our negotiations a bit."

"I'm not lying!" Vincente said. "I swear upon my mother's grave."

"Your mother's retired and on San Paul Prime," Mooney pointed out. After a moment of consideration, she nodded. "Sounds good to me, though. But if I find out you're lying to me..."

"You'll aim better," Vincente nodded. "I get it."

"Now tell me why you're destroying my bar," Mooney demanded in a curt tone. "And also why you even bothered coming back?"

"Well, I really wanted to pay you back the money I–"

"Horse shit," Mooney cut him off. "I can see the fear in your eyes. You didn't want to come back here to see me. Now tell me the truth."

"I need mercs," Vincente sighed. "About a dozen."

"For...?" she prodded.

"A job."

"I figured that, moron," Mooney scoffed. "For who?"

"Can't say."

"Government, eh? So that's how you can pay me back," Mooney nodded again and looked around. "Well, considering Jasmine probably crippled most of them, and killed their boss–"

"He grabbed a knife!" Jasmine protested.

"–your pickings are going to be a bit slim," Mooney finished. "I can get you six, probably, of my own men. Don't give me that look. I've hired better over the years. But they're good. Mean, but professional. Mostly."

"How much?" Vincente asked.

"Cover their ammo and equipment, and they're yours for fifty grand a head."

"That's extortion!" Vincente protested. "Fifteen, tops!"

"Thirty."

"Too high. My profit margin's already running thin, thanks to your five percent."

"Twenty-two, and that is my final offer."

"I can do that," Vincente nodded. "Shouldn't take more than two weeks, tops."

"Perfect," she grinned. "Now that we have that out of the way, we need to have a long talk. Darling."

Vincente heaved a mighty sigh. He almost wished that she had shot him.

****

"How'd it go?" Jasmine asked as Vincente came aboard the Fancy several hours later.

"Like ice skating up hill in the middle of a Medusan summer," he admitted. "That woman..."

"I got the mercs settled in and assigned berthing areas," Jasmine said as she handed over the ship's manifest to him. "We have provisions and gear all locked down in the storage area. I just need to let them know the rules of the ship and we'll be fine."

"Okay," Vincente grunted.

"I think we're about ready," Jasmine said.

"Did you take care of pre-flight and get air clearance for departure?" He asked. Seeing her nod, he grunted. "Okay, take care of our guests. I'll take us up into orbit, and then she's your bird."

Jasmine nodded again and headed towards the berthing area of the Fancy, where the mercenaries were putting their personal gear away in their small cabins. She cleared her throat loudly, ignoring a few appraising looks and a wolf whistle.

"Can I have your attention please?" she said. Once she was satisfied, she continued. "My name is Jasmine, and I'm the ship's pilot. I have a few rules that need to be obeyed, so listen up.

"First off, the engine room is off-limits. Our mechanic is skittish and peculiar, and hates dealing with people. Leave him alone, and he'll leave you alone. If you go down there, I will not hold him accountable for what he might do to you. I doubt he'll kill you, but he might hurt you. As I said, unpredictable. Plus, there are a ton of dangerous materials down there, including radioactive material. This ship is old, gentlemen, so please remember that.

"Secondly, stay out of the cockpit. There are delicate instruments up there, and that's my turf. I will hurt you if you go in there. That's not a threat, so don't roll your eyes at me, you overgrown lugheads. It's a promise. You've seen what I can do, so don't test it.

"Lastly, this job is dangerous. I can't go into specifics, due to who we're working for, but I can tell you this is a search and recovery, with the primary objective being retrieval of a ship's database. You're hired as muscle to keep us safe while we're on the planet. That's all you need to focus on, and worry about. Any questions? No? Good. Get your stuff stowed away, and prepare for departure. We'll be leaving in a bit."

She began to head back forward, but the mass of personal gear that the mercenaries had brought with them crowded the area. She waited for their nominal leader, Hector Cortez, to move a few things before she attempted to pass through the group again.

"Nice ass, babe," one of the mercs said as Jasmine walked near. "Name's Yolo. I could do things to you that haven't been written about yet."

"You don't want to do that," Jasmine said as she tried to work her way past the mercenary. Yolo's massive frame, however, blocked her. She stopped and looked up at the giant man.

"I got me a private cabin on this old tub," Yolo said as he leered down at her. "You know that, so why try to act surprised? Why don't we spend some downtime and get to know one another, eh?"

"I have to drive the ship," Jasmine said and offered the large mercenary a sweet, disarming smile. "And my cabin's bigger, so please move."

Yolo put his hand on her shoulder. "C'mon, what's the hurry? I–"

Jasmine grabbed the mercenary's wrist and twisted it behind his back. She threw him against the bulkhead with a surprising amount of force from someone so tiny, and drove her knee into the small of his back. Air whooshed out of him as she slammed his face two more times into the bulkhead before letting go and stepping away.

"Goddamned bitch!" Yolo roared as he struggled to regain his equilibrium. "I'm gonna–"

Jasmine whipped a gun out from the holster resting on her hip, her movements a blur to the naked eye. She pressed the barrel of her pistol against the man's head and pushed him back towards the bulkhead. He shut up instantly. She smiled again.

"Let's do science," she said and cocked the hammer of the gun. "Your head is four inches away from the bulkhead, which protects the ship from the vacuum of space normally. It is also a pressurized atmosphere in here, which keeps us comfortable and alive. We are about to exit the exosphere, which means that the air pressure outside is very low, almost like a vacuum. Now, the sealant skin between the bulkhead and outer hull of our ship can seal any gap in two seconds. The 750 grains of gunpowder I have in each .577 round can produce almost five tons of force from the muzzle alone. The shockwave can kill you, and the bullet definitely will. The science question is this: after I blow your head off and the round from this gun punches through the hull, can the vacuum of near-space suck out all your brains and blood so I won't have to clean it up later before the sealant skin activates? I've been dying to find out."

"Yolo, enough," Hector said from behind the diminutive pilot. "You heard the lady, and I'm pretty sure that she's not interested."

"Thanks for understanding," Jasmine said as she lowered her gun. She nodded at Hector. "I need to get up to the cockpit. Someone's going to have to fly this tub. You guys should try to get some rest."

Jasmine holstered her gun and skipped forward, leaving the mercenaries alone. Yolo rubbed his arm and watched her leave.

"Holy shit, boss," he whispered. "I think I'm in love."

Jasmine squeezed past Vincente's massive bulk as she entered the cockpit.

"Problems?" he asked her after casting a glance towards the aft of his ship.

"Not anymore," she replied as she sat down in the pilot's chair. She brought up her navigation guide. "Plotting a course to Gorgon IV now. ETA is... fourteen hours by skip speed, if we avoid the Chenier Cluster. Otherwise, we can pass near the cluster, and that means we'll be looking at two hours. I'd rather avoid that cluster, especially since one of the stars there has been creating massive flares the past eighteen months. It's a bit of a circuitous path to avoid it, but..."

"Sounds good to me," Vincente nodded. He eyed the screen. "How we looking for fuel?"

"We should top off before we hit the cluster," Jasmine stated. "I know, I know. We should be fine, but I don't want to get stuck out, wishing I had more fuel."

"Sounds good," Vincente nodded. "You got somewhere in mind?"

"The Wild Ones," Jasmine suggested. "They owe us a favor anyway."

"Owe you a favor," Vincente said. "They're not too fond of me."

"You know, you might want to stop making enemies," Jasmine said. "One of these days, someone's going to actually put a bullet in the right spot."

"You keep saying that."

"Doesn't make it any less true."

"Are you saying I don't have people skills? I'm a highly successful merchant."

"You get by," Jasmine allowed. "Though with the hauls we've had over the years, you should have been able to retire by now."

"I had... other commitments."

"Sure you did, boss." She punched in the new course. "Your commitment to alcohol is not something I'd shout out publicly. Okay, so the ETA to the Wild Ones is going to be five hours, then another eleven to Murder World. Yay, I can barely contain my enthusiasm."

"It'll be a breeze," Vincente said, though his voice lacked any conviction. "What could go wrong?"

"Oh, oh, no you didn't. Great, just fucking great. We're screwed now. Absolutely screwed. Thanks boss."

INTERLUDE II

"Please state your name for the record."

"Mooney."

The prosecutor sighed. "Your full legal name, please."

"Mooney Starchild Glow." A hint of grumpiness was in her tone.

"Thank you, Miss Glow. Now–"

"It's Mrs."

"I'm sorry?"

The woman in the dark suit scowled and brushed her bangs from her bright green eyes. She calmly smoothed out an imaginary wrinkle from her pleated jacket and picked at a stray thread, which had come from a seam. She stopped and looked back at the prosecutor.

"I'm a legally married woman. It's Mrs., if you will."

"I'm sorry," the prosecutor said. He looked at his screen and frowned. "I don't see any husband listed."

"That's because I haven't seen him in years," she replied. "Well, up until he showed up at my bar one day a few months back, asking for some kind of merc help. Rat bastard. Tore the bar up. Again."

"Wait," the prosecutor tapped a few notes onto his screen. He looked back her, incredulous. "Your husband is Vincente Huerta?"

"Unfortunately."

"I... see," the prosecutor's razor-thin smile was designed to make the woman across from him nervous. It faltered when he realized that it had no effect on her. He cleared his throat after an awkward moment of silence and continued. "Have you had any contact with your husband since the day you previously mentioned?"

"No."

"Has he attempted to make contact with you?"

"Isn't that the same thing?"

"Humor me."

"No, he hasn't," Mooney said. "He owes me for the damage to my bar. I want to see him. Five minutes should be all I'll need.

Maybe seven. I can get pretty creative with a knife, if I'm not rushed."

"Can you tell me what his state of mind was when he was at your bar the last time you saw him?"

"Scared. Terrified. Petrified. How many more synonyms are there for cowardly pus–"

"What was he scared of? The upcoming... mission? Did he talk about the job to you at all, how nervous he was or where it would be?"

"Hell no. He's never been afraid of a job, and he's as closed mouthed as they come. No, he was scared of me."

"I'm sorry?"

Mooney waved a hand dismissively. "He owed me a fortune, lied, stole, cheated, and lied some more to me over the years. Plus, he's a drunk. He should have been so frightened of me that he wouldn't step foot on that damn moon for years. I've got the only watering hole for five hundred kilometers in any direction. Only one worth a damn, at least. He knew that if he landed on the moon, I'd hear about it eventually. Damn fool."

"It sounds to me as though you still love him. Is your love for your... husband clouding your judgment today, perhaps influencing what you do and do not tell us?"

"I put a bullet in him, once. Would've made it two but he's quicker than he looks. That sound like love to you?"

"Uh..."

"So tell me," Mooney leaned closer to the prosecutor, her breasts pushing up and forming an impressive cleavage beneath the suit. She made sure his attention was diverted before she continued speaking. "What would make a man return when the woman he's coming back to has already tried to kill him once, and has a burning desire to finish the job proper this time?"

"Er..."

"You would have to be very desperate," she inhaled deeply, her eyes finally meeting those of the prosecutor's. "And a desperate man is a dangerous one."

CHAPTER FOUR

Vincente wasn't a social creature by nature. It wasn't that he hated every known life form in explored space, it was just that every time he tried to get along with them, they usually went for a weapon. His mother had always called him a sweet boy, but even then, the other kids in his old neighborhood tended to want to fight with him. Still, he didn't want to drink alone, and wanted to get a feel for the mercenaries that he'd hired from Mooney.

Their leader, Hector, whom he recognized from the files on the men Jasmine had given him that he'd halfway scanned over, sat in the Fancy's cargo bay. He was using a crate of munitions as a makeshift place to rest his impressive bulk. The man was cleaning a rather deadly looking rifle as Vincente entered the bay. Two more of the mercenaries were present. One was a ratty little man with sharp, bird like features. Vincente figured if the man's nose was any pointier, he wouldn't even classify as human. He was puffing on a cigarette, in direct violation of regulations, which monitored interstellar travel. Vincente had done it himself in the past, so there was no point in picking an argument over something so trivial. The Fancy's atmospheric scrubbers were more than up to the task of dealing with the situation. The other mercenary was an ordinary looking fellow with a mop of thick brown hair atop his head. The tail end of a nasty scar peeked out from beneath it, just above his right eye. He stood, propped up against one of the bay's walls, reading what appeared to be an actual book. All three of the men stopped what they were doing and turned to stare at him as they noticed his presence.

"Hi," Vincente hit them with his charm, waving a hand at them in greeting. "Figured at least some of you guys would be here, you know, stretching your legs and all that. The cabins on this ship can feel a bit cramped."

"You have to be Vincente," Hector growled, snapping his weapon back together.

Vincente did a double take, re-appraising the mercenary leader as he wracked his brain for a witty come back, ending up with "What makes you say that?"

"I want to kick in your teeth already," Hector chuckled. "I've been told you have somewhat of a reputation."

"And you'd be Hector," Vincente said, trying and failing to save at least some face.

"Don't be too impressed by his knowing who you are," the little, ratty man cut in. "Ms. Mooney told us you'd be old, fat, and annoying."

"She did, did she?" The words flew from Vincente's mouth before he could stop them. Thankfully, even if the mercenaries were loyal to Mooney, they seemed willing to give him a chance before they gutted him and flung his corpse out the airlock of his own ship. Vincente shook his head and got a grip on his rampant thoughts. "Forget Ms. Mooney. You're working for me now. Sort of. You want to introduce yourselves, or should I just start making up names for you?"

Hector rose. He didn't offer Vicente his hand. Instead, he nodded at the other two men. "That there is Shannon and Melts. Shannon is our field tech, Melts is just another grunt with delusions of scholardom."

"Hey now!" Melts shouted, slamming shut the book he'd been reading.

"I see you come bearing gifts," Shannon said, gesturing towards the bottle and plastic cups that Vincente carried.

Vincente handed out the cups to the three mercenaries, keeping one for himself. "Best way to get to know someone fast is to get completely and thoroughly trashed with them," he smiled. "Assuming, of course, you guys can hold your drink. You start shooting up my cargo bay, or take a shot at me, and I might be obliged to take some serious offense to that."

An hour later, Vincente staggered out of the cargo bay feeling good about himself and the mercenaries. Sure, they were a rough sort of people, but these guys seemed all right. If these three were a sample of what all of them that came abroad were like, they were going to be just fine to work with. Hector really knew how to drink and Melts was a lot more than a pretend scholar. Even drunk, the guy could quote Shakespeare and Marlowe and eloquently compare their styles with the best of them. He was doing a one man Macbeth while countering every other line with Doctor Faustus by the time they hit the bottom of the bottle Vincente had taken to them. It had been uproariously funny to the drunken men.

Shannon, however, was a creepy sort of man. He would sip his drink, staying sober while the others had descended into drunkenness, watching the others with narrow eyes. Vincente made a mental note to keep an eye on him, and then promptly forgot it, as the bottle grew emptier. With any sort of luck, he should have plenty of time to sleep off his "getting to know one another" party with the mercenaries before they met up with the Wild Ones. If they didn't, maybe it was for the best. Like dealing with Mooney, dealing with the Wild Ones was always a headache of its own for him, just not as deadly of one.

Usually. They were a tad bit unpredictable at times.

As he headed for his quarters, a big man with a grim scowl on his face, approached him from the opposite direction he was headed. The man was one of Hector's mercenaries, Vincente was certain. He certainly had never hired someone that size before. He was huge and had the mass of a moving wall of concrete. As they reached the point of passing one another, the man extended an incredibly thick, muscled arm, blocking Vincente's path. Vincente looked at the giant towering over him as the man asked, "You're the captain, ain't ya?"

Vincente, completely nonplussed, answered in a slurred voice. "I am, I think. Yes, I am. You got a problem with that, mister... walking wall?"

A small part of Vincente's brain tried to warn him against pissing off people bigger than he was, but that part was overruled by drunken bravado and sheer stupidity, courtesy of the liquid courage he had poured down his gullet. Thankfully, the giant chuckled instead of picking him up and breaking him in half.

"You got one fine pilot," the giant commented. "Women like her are rare. I hope you appreciate that."

"Always," Vincente grinned from ear to ear. God favors drunks and fools. "And you are?"

"You can call me Yolo."

"Sure thing," Vincente nodded, wishing he were already in his bed and dead to the world. "Thanks for sharing that. I'll be sure to let Jasmine know she has a fan down here in gung-ho land."

Yolo removed his arm from Vincente's path. "You do that now."

"Oh, I will," Vincente called over his shoulder as he hurriedly stumbled on along the corridor. The walls kept moving on him and he was having trouble keeping the right wall on the right side. "Count on it."

Vincente finally made it to his quarters and fell into his bed. At least this time I made it onto the bed, he remembered thinking as his head hit the pillow. He was out as fast as a light being turned off.

****

Vincente was proud of himself. He was not only awake with the miracle of a fresh stim pumping through his body, though it hadn't been a full twelve hours since the last one, but he was as ready as he was ever going to be to deal with the Wild Ones. He swaggered onto the bridge where Jasmine still sat at the Fancy's helm.

She took one glance and tore into him. "I told you to wait twelve hours. Those stims aren't something you want to mess around with. What the hell, Vincente? You trying to give yourself an aneurysm? I want to get paid, and if you die, I don't. Jesus, you stink. Have you showered since we left the bar? Oh, God, have you even changed your shirt?"

Vincente dismissively waved a hand at her as he took his seat. "I'll be fine. I'll blend right in with the natives. We there yet?"

"Just dropped out of Null Space," she confirmed. "We're closing with the Wild Ones' station now. Their portside thrusters are firing radically, but I think that's just because they're too stoned to realize that their artificial gravity still works. I can bring us in without a problem though. Their axial spin is manageable."

"Good, let's get this over with."

The Wild Ones were human, but they chose to live on the fringes of civilized space. Their proximity to the Zebulun Hegemony didn't bother them at all. Of course, it could be argued that nothing bothered them. The Zebulun were unlikely to waste the effort to come after them, even in the war-like state they always seemed to be in. The Wild Ones were a breakaway group of freaks, as Vincente saw them, who believed in crazy things like animal spirits, ritualistic body scarring, and partying to an extreme that made even him uncomfortable. While he sometimes bent or broke the law, the Wild Ones made it their way of life. They didn't see time as the more sophisticated societies did. They lived very much in the now. To them, each moment was all that mattered. That made them about the most unpredictable bunch of weirdoes in the galaxy to deal with. Jasmine seemed to have a way with the Wild Ones, though. When they'd last passed through, the Wild Ones had almost committed mass suicide when they realized she wasn't staying.

Plus, their leader did owe Jasmine a favor for the supply of illegal bio-gel she'd slipped them from the cargo they'd been hauling at the time. Vincente didn't even want to contemplate what the Wild Ones had used the stuff for, and Jasmine had stayed mum about it in the ensuing months since. In any case, if something did go wrong, they had the mercenaries on broad. Added firepower was always a good thing.

The station didn't have a lot of modern equipment, so Jasmine was docking them manually. With another pilot at the Fancy's controls, Vincente might have worried but Jasmine was an even a better pilot than she was a fighter. The ship aligned its self gracefully and clamped into place on the station's outer ring.

Vincente activated the internal comm. "This is the captain. We've now docked at the Coyote Station. Jasmine and I will be leaving the ship briefly to oversee our refueling. I want everyone else to stay on board. Kamol, be ready to receive the fuel."

****

"You ready for this?" Jasmine asked as the two of them stood in front of the airlock that led onto Coyote Station.

"No, not even close. Will you shut up and open the blasted door already?" Vincente complained.

Jasmine smiled as she punched the keys on the door's pad. The thick door slid sideways, disappearing into its frame. As it did so, the smell of Coyote Station came rushing over Vincente. He gagged, raising a hand to cover his nose and mouth. The station's air stank of unwashed bodies, urine, alcohol, and burning incense with subtle undertone of tobacco and rotting flesh.

A man with long hair tied in dreadlocks sat just outside the station's docking lock as they entered. There was no doubt that he was flying high as he groggily looked at them. The pupils of his eyes were dilated and his movements were sluggish and careful. A thick, hand-rolled cigarette dangled loosely from his lips. A quick whiff told Vincente that tobacco was not what the man was smoking.

His speech was so slurred and slow that Vincente didn't have a clue what the man said as he spoke to them. Vincente glanced over at Jasmine.

"He asked if we had a smoke," Jasmine explained with a shrug. "I think he forgot about the one he already has. That smells like some potent stuff."

"Wild One security," Vincente shook his head ruefully. "Got to love it."

The man said something else. Jasmine translated his words a second time. "He says the Big Kahuna is expecting us. We're to go on ahead. He'll catch up later."

"Yeah, right," Vincente snorted.

They left the man sitting where he was as he waved after them in an exaggerated friendly manner. The station's corridors were filled with various bits of litter and human waste. If one judged the Wild Ones solely on their security, work ethic, and hygiene, their society came across as a group of lazy children not even able to clean up after themselves. However, they were some of the fiercest fighters in the known galaxy, when not completely blitzed on relaxants and downers. Their passion for bloodshed was matched only by their passion for partying, and one oftentimes led to the other. They made excellent irregular troops, if you could put up with their outright lack of discipline and their general bloodthirsty nature. Though the Wild Ones were competent with modern weaponry, they preferred to use vibro-blades and their fists. There was a certain pleasure, they claimed, in feeling the warm blood of one's enemy spraying over you as their life ended at your hand.

Personally, Vincente always suspected the grease and grime in the station kept the rounds from chambering properly in their guns.

As they passed through the Coyote Station's winding mass of corridors towards the Big Kahuna's Great Hall, several Wild Ones approached Jasmine. They greeted her with offers of food, drugs and sex. She politely turned down all of them, men and women alike. Those who refused to be denied her company were slammed into the station's bulkhead and ended up limp, unconscious bodies on the refuse-covered metal floor. They would brag about it later, undoubtedly. He grinned but said nothing, though he did wonder if she would eventually end up being revered as a goddess by these people.

She certainly had a way with people.

The Big Kahuna Great Hall was a wide, spacious bay-type area. At its far end sat the Big Kahuna's throne and the man they wanted to see, Kahuna Numero Uno Ragara. Ragara sat high upon his throne – in reality, an old starship command chair mounted on some pylons which had been hastily welded together, with fake flowers melted onto the top of the back rest and some plushy stuffed animals between each – surrounded by a half dozen women in various states of undress. Vincente found it particularly hard not to stare at one brunette who wore nothing more than a stained white tank top. Rows of scars covered her legs from her ankles to her thighs. He wondered if they were self-inflicted as was often the custom with the Wild Ones, or if they had a special meaning. Apparently, he stared too long at the fetching savage woman because Jasmine's elbow collided with his ribcage.

"Hey!" Vincente started, but Jasmine shushed him. Big Kahuna Ragara had risen from his throne and was walking to meet them.

Ragara spread his hands before him in an over the top gesture of greeting. He smiled broadly, revealing crooked teeth and quite a few gaps in them. One did not become Big Kahuna through gentle means. "Welcome once more to Coyote Station, Ms. Jasmine. It is very good to see you again. Your captain? Not so much."

Much to Vincente's shock, Jasmine bowed to the poorly dressed elder. "Greetings to you as well, Most High One. We have come to purchase fuel for our vessel, the Fancy, to take pleasure in your company. We will not trouble you long."

Ragara made a clicking sound with his tongue and the remains of his yellowed teeth. "To hear that you will not be staying to indulge in our hospitality saddens me, but I can see that your Captain Vincente wants to get straight to business as usual. What have you brought with you this time to trade?"

"Actually, I was hoping to buy the fuel outright," Vincente answered. Negotiations with the Wild Ones was always a learning experience.

"Prosperous times are upon you, I see," Ragara snapped his fingers and one of his women hurried forward to offer Vincente and Jasmine mugs containing a thick, greenish liquid. They accepted the offered drinks as Vincente tried to slosh his around to see if it was something alive. He didn't recognize the smell, though it wasn't quite unpleasant. He took a cautious sip and managed, with some difficulty, to keep from making a disgusted face. Some plants shouldn't be mixed with alcohol, especially coca leaf and mint.

"We're prepared to offer you fifty thousand credits for the fuel," Jasmine said bluntly, cutting to the chase.

Vincente felt his stomach turn as he thought about the amount of money. The expenses of this job were reducing his profit margin at every turn.

"Done!" Ragara exclaimed. Vincente mentally cursed. He should have had her start the bid lower, haggle a bit. He probably could have shaved ten thousand off the final price. "I shall have my men bring it to your ship at once!"

"Thank you, Most High One," Jasmine flashed a smile at the old man. Vincente was surprised she didn't bat her eyelashes at him too. Her smile was full of lewd promises and other meanings. He prayed it was all just an act. Sometimes, with Jasmine, you just never knew.

After the refusal of several more attempts at Wild One hospitality, including an offer for a brawl in the hall, which Jasmine really wanted to take part in, they returned to the Fancy. Hector was standing outside the airlock, arguing with the stoned sentry about firepower versus a vibro-blade. The Wild Ones sentry was determined to make his point, though the two mercenaries seemed to be handling it far more diplomatically than Vincente would have. Jasmine called out to the sentry, who jumped back and slid the knife he had been holding out moments before into a sheath on his leg. He put on an air of innocence, which might have fooled a five year old, if the child was especially gullible.

"Fuel, paid for already to the Big Kahuna," Jasmine said. "Be a sweetie and fetch us the tube, will you?"

The Wild One hastily complied. Vincente looked at her.

"You're not human," he told her.

"You just don't get them," she countered. "It's a nice feeling when you're dealing with a culture whose mantra revolves around sex, drugs and warfare. Simpler, you know? Easier to get through to them. Plus, they respect strength."

"Go help Kamol with the fuel lines," he said, shaking his head. He looked at the two mercenaries. "You guys were supposed to stay on board."

"I've dealt with Wild Ones before," Hector offered in way of explanation. "Had one work for me, actually."

"Besides, your engineer is creepy," Shannon added. Vincente blinked at that. He doubted that the diminutive mercenary had room to call anybody creepy, much less a tiny alien.

"Never dealt with the Lorn before?" Vincente asked. Seeing the two men shake their heads, he grunted. "All right, just don't critique his engine or the engine room, or the way he does stuff. He's very literal, like all Lorn are, so if you say something as a joke or a sarcastic reply, he's going to take it seriously and, if it's bad enough, probably try to hurt you."

"He's three feet tall with three skinny arms," Shannon complained. "What's the worst thing he can do? Pinch me to death?"

"It's your funeral," Vincente shrugged. "Since you're here, go help Jasmine and Kamol with the fuel lines. I want to get going as soon as possible."

"Sure," Hector nodded. "Shannon, go grab Melts and help out. Tell Yolo to stay out of the way." The short mercenary nodded and scampered off. Hector glanced at Vincente. "Great man in a fight, Yolo is. Don't let him touch anything else, though. It tends to end up broken. He once fried a space station's database somehow while ordering a drink. The station tech teams had been so impressed that they banned him from ever setting foot there again."

"Good to know," Vincente mentally filed that little bit of information away for future use. There was little desire for him to watch his ship being turned into a smoldering wreck because some mercenary was bad luck around electronics. He followed Hector back inside the Fancy, where he found Shannon trying to help Kamol finish the fueling. It did not appear to be going well.

"No, I don't think you understand," Shannon said. "If you keep the valve regulators half-open, you can improve efficiency by about fifteen percent. Sure, you run the risk of overflow, but these tubes are designed to prevent that, so you'd really have to try to screw it up."

"Hatcha torflin vath conna melandishrk!" Kamol said, his tone rising. The alien's hair on his head was standing on end, which Vincente knew to be a sign of his growing agitation towards the mercenary. Kamol crossed two of his three arms behind his head, his third arm scratching his chin. His black eyes glared at Shannon as he continued. "Maks don roun kurtsch dou?"

"I don't know what the hell you just said, but I'm sure that you're limiting yourself by not running those regulators the way I said," Shannon argued.

"Charka dou?"

"No idea, but I know I'm right."

"Charka dou?"

"If you're trying to say that you're wrong, then yeah. Charka dou."

Kamol suddenly shoved the mercenary with his third arm. Shannon stumbled back a step, recovering before he could fall down and look foolish. He took a step towards the engineers.

"Watch yourself, asshole," Shannon growled. "I'm doing your job."

"Charka dou?"

"Up yours," Shannon said and took a swing at the alien.

Kamol was ready, however, and despite their short stature, Lorn were exceptionally strong and dexterous. He weaved between two quick jabs that Shannon followed up with and slammed the open palm of his third hand directly into the mercenary's chin. Dazed, Shannon stumbled back and bumped the bulkhead. He stepped away and tried to get to the center of the room. Kamol screamed a Lorn war cry and launched himself into the air, arms akimbo as he flew across the room.

"Oh God!" Shannon nearly screamed as Kamol landed atop him. The small but heavy Lorn pushed the mercenary to the ground, using two of his three arms to pin Shannon's to his side. The third chest-centered arm began repeatedly punching the thin mercenary hard in the face.

"Dou rema part osch? Dou rema part osch?" Kamol repeated each time his fist connected with Shannon's face. The mercenary already had some blood trickling from multiple small cuts on his face, and his bottom lip had been fattened.

"Get him off! Help!"

"This is amusing," Yolo said, standing off to the side. His massive arms were folded across his chest. He looked over at the captain. "What's he saying? The little guy, I mean?"

"He's saying, 'Why do you make me hit you?' over and over, I think," Vincente said. "Lorn verb tenses get weird when they're angry, Kamol more so than others."

"Huh," Yolo snorted. "Funny."

"Help me!" Shannon screeched.

"Fine," Vincente rolled his eyes. "Kamol, get off him!"

"Schash hinde partour!" More punches rained down upon the helpless mercenary's face.

"He didn't mean to insult your techniques," Vincente tried to placate him. "He just thought he might be able to show you a different way. Doesn't mean it's better, just different."

"Karltom dou?" The punching stopped.

"Yeah, different, not better," Vincente had the alien's full attention at last. "Get this fuel line off our ship so we can get out of here, Kamol."

"Sazhu." Kamol let go of the mercenary and lifted him back up, his skinny arms surprisingly strong. He patted Shannon's hip, and the mercenary shied away. The little alien scampered off to finish his job, leaving the bloodied man behind.

Shannon wiped some blood from his face. He gave Vincente a dirty look, which the captain easily shrugged off.

"I warned you not to mess with him," Vincente reminded. "Lorn are pretty strong."

Jasmine walked into the bay and stopped. She looked at Shannon, then at Vincente before she threw her hands up into the air. She exhaled in exasperation.

"Oh, sure, beat the hell out of the little guy, but I can't play with the Wild Ones for a bit! You're such an ass, Vincente!" she stormed back to the cockpit. Vincente and Yolo shared a look. She yelled at him from the cockpit. "Asshole!"

"Wait... what the hell did I do?"

"Oh, yeah, I'm definitely in love."

CHAPTER FIVE

Gorgon IV was an ugly world, with a nebulous storm system, which made the upper ionosphere look like pea soup. Vincente stared at the planet's image on the Fancy's view screen. There were no beautiful green, blue, and whites like Earth. Gorgon IV's entire atmosphere and surface were various shades of green and grey, while lightning-like bolts of energy danced inside its nearly complete sheath of clouds.

The Fancy had settled into orbit around the planet nearly twenty minutes ago and Jasmine was still fighting with the ship's sensors to get a good read of the planetary surface below. After a few more minutes of futile efforts, Jasmine threw up her hands in disgust.

"Forget it, boss," she told him, "The only way we're going to get a lock on that research vessel we're after is to go into that mess–" she indicated the highly charged storm masses raging across the world's surface¬ "–and hope the ship's sensors function better at closer range."

Vincente leaned forward in his command chair. He frowned. "You really think that's a good idea? The atmosphere looks pretty rough from where I'm sitting."

"If you got a better idea, I'm open to it," Jasmine's voice was full of frustrated rage. She was still mad at him for not allowing her to fight with the Wild Ones, he guessed.

"Nope, I got nothing," he admitted. "You can't detect anything down there?"

"Oh, I can tell there's a lot of rocks and sand," Jasmine chuckled darkly. "Some small bodies of water, and one hell of a polar icecap in the southerly polar region. The problem's not just the atmosphere. Underneath the sand covering, most of the planet is large deposits of some type of metal. No idea what kind. Never seen anything like it, but it's mildly radioactive. Between its interference, and the energy bouncing around the clouds, getting a solid lock on a crashed ship is like digging for a needle in a haystack."

Vincente frowned and rubbed at his cheeks. "You'd think a military ship like the one we're after would have some kind of emergency beacon." He was beginning to realize that he had seriously undercharged for the job at hand.

"Wouldn't matter," Jasmine explained. "Once we enter the atmosphere, the comm system will be essentially inoperative. All that interference will flood any outgoing or incoming channels. That includes the pulse of an emergency beacon. Of course, since this 'research vessel' was spying on the Zebulun anyway, it possibly didn't even have one."

"How about life forms? Did you try scanning for those?" He asked. Jasmine looked insulted. Vincente cleared his throat. "It was just a suggestion, ya know? Guess I should have known you tried that, too."

"The risk to the Fancy should be minimal if we go in. The lightning may look like Hell, but based on the sensor data, it's more bark than bite, I think."

Vincente grunted. He didn't relish the idea of taking his ship into the mess below, but there didn't appear to be another choice. He mulled his other options, but there seemed to be none that ended up with him being paid. Finally, he nodded. "Okay, if you're sure, take us in."

As the Fancy's engines powered up for the ship's descent, he opened the internal comm channel. "Hector, get your boys ready. We're going in. In and out, no muss, no fuss. This should be a quick extraction if we do this right."

"You got it," Hector's voice answered before Vincente killed the comm and refocused his attention on the view screen. The plan was pretty simple as things went. Find the downed spy ship. Send in the mercs to get the data from their computers. Get the hell out of Dodge. Get paid, and paid well.

The Fancy swept downward, trading the darkness of space for the raging fury of Gorgon IV's atmosphere. Vincente felt the ship lurch as the air pressure outside began to grow unstable, the pressure of the storm changing the air by the second. He could hear the energy of the atmosphere crackle and hiss as bolts of it struck the Fancy's hull. Jasmine kept the ship high above the world's surface and its speed a good clip for a fast, flyby recon with the sensors extended to their maximum range.

"What the–" she never got to finish.

Vincente recognized the tone of confusion and terror in his pilot's voice, one he never thought he'd hear. She whirled around in her chair, her mouth in the process of forming a scream as something shifted in the atmosphere outside the hull. A bolt of energy as powerful as a warship's main cannons slammed into the Fancy. Vincente was flung forward. He thudded onto the floor, rolling across the bridge, as Jasmine clung to the armrests of her own chair, teeth gritted tightly. Even as he struggled to get up, he saw that she had managed to right herself at her station, her safety harnesses holding her in place for the time being. Alarm klaxons were blaring all over the ship. The main lights had gone dark, replaced by the softer red tones of the emergency ones. The lights that he never wanted to see. Diving for his seat, Vincente made it, getting strapped in himself, just before a second blast rocked the ship. His thumb stabbed the internal comm switch.

"If you aren't already holding onto something, I suggest that you do!" he shouted. Glancing at Jasmine where she sat at the helm locked in losing battle with the Fancy's controls, he added, "It looks like we're going to be experiencing some extreme turbulence on the way down."

"The scan of the surface!" Jasmine cried, too busy to look in his direction as she screamed, "It set off some kind of reaction with the energy in the atmosphere! The energy out there has picked up by a magnitude of ten!"

"Siah cargna!" Kamol's voice rang out over the comm from engineering. "Tawatcha leed wog!"

"Kamol says we can't take too many more hits like that," Vincente shouted.

"I speak Lorn, you fucking halfwit!" Jasmine snapped. "I'm taking us down. We have to get out of these clouds!"

Vincente nodded, trusting Jasmine's judgment and ignoring her outburst. The second blast of energy had toasted a bunch of the ship's systems, and the faint smell of tangy smoke filled the air. An electrical fire somewhere, Vincente recognized. Exposed wiring dangled from collapsed sections of the bridge's ceiling above them. As bad as things were, Vincente thought as he shot a glance at a man-sized chunk of the ceiling that had caved in near the bridge's entrance, they could be a lot worse.

"We're all going to die!" came a cry from the mercenary berthing space. It sounded like Yolo, but he couldn't be certain.

A third bolt of energy crashed from the clouds into the Fancy. As it struck the hull, somehow, it bled directly into the ship's systems this time, running along the power conduits. Several consoles on the bridge exploded as the energy reached them. He saw that Jasmine had freed herself of the safety harness of the pilot seat. She leaped away from the controls there just as they also went up in flames.

Something large crashed down from the ceiling of the cockpit. Vincente yelped as a large chunk of electronics and heavy plastic narrowly missed him. Outside, the sky turned white, then beige. It took him a second to realize that he was looking at the surface of the Gorgon IV and they had passed through the cloud cover.

"Hey, look, we made it." He then realized that the ground was rushing up to meet them much faster than he was comfortable with.

"Brace for impact!" she howled as Vincente felt something heavy and solid strike his head. Everything was suddenly spinning, and he wasn't sure if it was him or the Fancy. Around him, the universe went black.

****

Vincente woke up in the Fancy's small medical bay. He lay stretched out on one of its autodoc beds. The room was filled with a dim light, but the color was wrong. His head ached. The fingers of his right hand rose to glide over the fabric of the bandage covering his forehead.

Jasmine sat nearby, allowing the robotic doctor unit that was attached to the med-bay's ceiling to work on her hands. Vincente could smell the faint odor of charred skin from where he lay, though her burns didn't appear too bad. One of the mercs lay in the bed beside his. Vincente couldn't remember the man's name.

He wasn't one of the three he had gotten wasted with before they'd reached Gorgon IV, and he wasn't nearly large enough to be Yolo.

The mercenary appeared to be in pretty bad shape. A piece of the Fancy's interior walls protruded from the man's chest like the shaft of a spear. The wound around the spear was a jagged mess of torn flesh and the man's skin was pale from blood loss. Vincente wasn't a doctor but his instincts told him that the mercenary was a goner no matter what the autodoc did.

Emergency power must've been restored somehow, a small part of his brain that wasn't in pain observed.

Hector and Yolo stood near the med-bay's door. There was no sign of Kamol or the other two mercenaries. Vincente groaned and tried to sit up. The world spun around him and he slumped back onto the bed.

"You screamed," Vincente managed to spit out through his dry mouth.

"You're awake," Jasmine commented. "And I never screamed."

"How bad?" Vincente croaked.

"You or the ship?" Jasmine asked.

"Give me the good news first," Vincente told her.

"You've got a mild concussion from a piece of shrapnel that grazed you. Minor lacerations, nothing the autodoc couldn't handle. You also got some scalp glued back into place, but the scar should be small. As much as you may regret it later, you're going to live."

"And the Fancy?"

Jasmine took a deep breath. "Kamol is trying to breathe some life back into her, but she took a beating. The atmospheric energy overloaded her systems, shorting out the circuitry in the cockpit. Of course, the crash that followed finished the job. I doubt she'll ever see space again, no matter what Kamol says," Jasmine paused and smiled sadly. "Luckily, he's blaming you, not me, for the crash. He's pretty livid about the whole thing, as you can imagine."

"Great," Vincente muttered. "You were the one who said it was safe."

"I said that it was probably safe," she reminded him.

"What else?"

"One bit of good news," Jasmine flashed him a grin. "Well, two. First, Kamol got emergency power up, so we can at least use the autodocs. The beam weapons were fried, but I doubt we want to use them in an atmosphere like this anyway. I was also able to locate another ship on the surface as we went down. It's not too far from our current position, actually. Whether or not it's the ship we were sent after, who knows? Regardless, it might be in better shape than the Fancy. Or at the very least provide Kamol with some of the parts he's saying he needs."

"What about Gorgon IV?" Vincente asked.

"You should call it what it is, Vincente," Hector snarled bitterly. "Murder World."

"The air here is breathable and the energy spikes seemed to be contained in the upper atmosphere," Jasmine ignored the mercenary's anger. Apparently, she had been keeping the peace while he was unconscious. "Just like the sensors indicated before everything went to Hell, the planet out there is mostly sand and rock. The temps run about equivalent to an Earth desert. The temps shouldn't drop too much at night, so there's that. Wouldn't want to stay outside for long, but I think we can manage the hike to that other ship I mentioned."

"Any indigenous life?"

Hector answered, his voice a little more mellow than before. "Not that we've seen so far. The crash left some rather gaping holes in this ship's hull. I've had Melts, Shannon, and Jacob standing watch at them. So far, all they've seen is blowing sand and lightning up in the clouds. Shannon thinks that the crash scared off any life, but the predators – if there are any – will come back eventually."

"We're right on the border of the planet's equatorial and transitional zones," Jasmine said as soon as the mercenary leader stopped. "Hot and humid, thanks to that cloud cover. Not sure why there isn't a lot of vegetation, but Kamol thinks that it's due to the strange metals in the ground."

"Good work, everybody," Vincente smiled despite the pounding in his head. He closed his eyes and rested his head. "Get your men over to that other ship and check it out. Take Kamol as well. If you can drag him away from the Fancy for long enough, that is."

"No way. Nope," Jasmine got up and walked over to his bed. She poked him in the chest with a finger, hard. "You're not staying here, Vincente. You're the one who accepted this job. Get your butt out of that bed and get geared up, because you'll be going with them."

Vincente blinked and stared at his pilot. "I'm the captain of this ship, and I am staying with her. That's what the captain does. Stay with his ship."

"Not today," Jasmine jerked him to his feet. He stumbled but managed to stay upright. The painful throbbing in his head intensified. "I'm staying, you're going. Deal with it, boss. I'm the only one other than Kamol who knows enough about engineering to help get the Fancy space-worthy again, since you're taking him with you."

He knew better than to argue with Jasmine when she got like this. Vincente sighed and relented, a little. "Fine. You heard the lady, gentlemen," he said to the mercenaries, "We're moving out. Make sure you're geared up properly, including body armor."

"Body armor?" Hector asked.

"Better safe than sorry," Vincente shrugged. He then had a thought. "Crap, I don't think my armor fits anymore."

"Get moving, chubby," Jasmine ordered her boss. He sighed and walked to his cabin.

Twenty minutes and a lot of swearing later, Vincente finally had his body armor strapped on and secured. Hector met him in the passageway. The mercenary had attached various weapons to his armor with quick-release mechanisms, though he had not put on a tactical helmet. Vincente felt foolish wearing his, but declined taking it off. He silently followed the mercenary.

Hector's heavy boots clanged against the floor of the corridor as Hector led him to a torn up section of the Fancy's hull. Melts stood near the opening, an automatic rifle clutched in his hands. The mercenary scholar was looking out of the large, gaping hole for any sign of danger. Vincente peered over his shoulder to get his first real look at Gorgon IV, but his vision was blocked. A hazy, smoke like fog drifted into the corridor from the hole in the hull, dispersing into the ship's internal atmosphere.

"Your alien was able to rig up some integrity fields for the spots like this, but that stuff," Melts nodded at the fog, "seeps through anyhow. As far as we can tell, it's not toxic or anything. It did kill the reactive skin protecting the outer hole, so I guess your pilot won't get to test her theory anytime soon."

Shannon and another mercenary approached them the hole from the other end of the corridor, opposite from the way he and Hector had come to join them. Hector had called them from their own guard posts.

"This is Jacob," Hector introduced the captain to the final mercenary.

"I don't like leaving the ship like this," Shannon said as soon as Hector had finished.

"Me either," Hector checked the magazine of the rifle he carried. "But Yolo will be staying with the civvies, and that pilot is no slouch when it comes to bringing the pain and destruction. Besides, we won't be gone long."

"Hey!" Melts looked around and frowned. "Where's your alien, Vincente?"

Vincente shrugged. "Thought you guys were bringing him."

Shannon stifled a laugh as Jacob went red. "I tried to," Jacob confessed. "He went wild and started cursing, I think. All I know is, when he started swinging a wrench at my head, I decided that it was someone else's problem. So I left him where he was."

Vincente laughed. "Sounds like him. Smart call on leaving him be."

"He gave me this though," Jacob handed a tablet to Vincente. "I think it's some sort of list of things he wants us to bring back if we can find them. I've never heard of some of these parts. What type of ship is this, exactly?"

"Tramp freighter," Vincente lied easily.

"So does it look good?" Hector asked.

"Anyone know what a flux capacitor is?" Vincente joked, scanning over the list.

None of the mercenaries was amused, Hector least of all. "You got it then? You can make sense of that list?"

"Tough crowd," Vincente muttered, chuckling to himself, then went serious. "Yeah, I got it. Jasmine may be the pilot, and Kamol the engineer, but this is my ship. I'm not an idiot, you know?"

Vincente could have sworn he heard Shannon whisper, "You could have fooled me," but he chose to ignore the remark.

"Okay then," Hector barked and chambered a round into his rifle. "Let's get moving. If that crap out there is what passes for daytime here, I do not want to see what this planet's night is like."

Jacob took point as the others followed him out of the ship. Melts brought up the rear of the squad with Vincente, Hector, and Shannon in between them. All of the mercenaries were armed to the teeth, but Vincente had refused the offer of a rifle. However, he did carry his pistol holstered on his hip.

He was confident. He was not a fool, though.

****

Jasmine had been correct about the planet being a lot of rock and sand. The squad had been on the move for over an hour now and the sand under the squad's feet still stretched ceaselessly on into the horizon. Here and there, a clump of black rocks, covered in sharp, jutting points, rose from the desert. There was no plant life that Vincente saw. This place was the epitome of the word barren.

Sweat dripped from Vincente's brow and soaked through his clothes. There was no real sunlight. The planet's messed up atmosphere saw to that, but the heat was nigh unbearable all the same. He had known that the greenhouse effect would be bad, but he was caught completely unprepared for the staggering amount of humidity in the air. He was on the verge of asking Hector if the squad could take a break when they spotted the ship up ahead. There was no doubt it was a human vessel, or at least, it had been. It resembled a class of transport that had been decommissioned from active service a decade ago, he recognized. There was a good possibility he had piloted a similar vessel long ago.

The squad picked up their pace, hurrying on towards the ship. The vessel was in worse shape than the Fancy. He had definitely piloted one of those ships when he first had gotten started in the independent shipping industry. Vincente realized that the entire forward section of the ship was simply gone. The transport must have broken apart during its crash, he figured. It made sense. An older class of ship like this one wouldn't have the hull strength of a newer class like the Fancy. Plus, he had no idea what had brought the vessel down in the first place.

Hector and his men did their thing as the squad reached the ship. Vincente waited outside with Hector while the Melts and Shannon entered the ship and Jacob swept on around its corner to recon the area on its other exterior side.

When Melts and Shannon re-emerged from the ship, they were frazzled. "Sir," Melts addressed Hector. "I think you need to see what's in there. It looks like some of the ship's crew survived, at least for a while. One section was welded shut and then caved in from the outside. There's a lot of interior damage that doesn't appear to have come from its crash. Looks more like someone fought a war in there."

"Wait here with the captain" Hector ordered Shannon, then turned and followed Melts back into the ship.

"So, uh, was there anything useful in there?" Vincente asked.

"How would I know?" Shannon answered. "You're the one with the list. If you mean stuff like rations, water, ammo... then hell no. From all the casings on the floors, it looks like whoever was on that ship when it went down shot their way through their whole supply. As to the rest, it must have been in the forward part of this ship. This mess here is mostly just personal quarters and one freaking huge cargo bay that's empty. They must have been headed back home after unloading somewhere when they ended up here."

The two men stood in silence for a few minutes until it seemed Shannon couldn't take it anymore. "I tell you, man. It's spooky in there."

"I thought you soldier guys didn't get spooked," Vincente taunted the little man.

"Up yours, you asshole," Shannon snarled at him. "Something, and I do mean something, got onto that ship after it crashed and dragged everyone on board out. There are blood trails leading from the areas where it looked like the crew tried to hold out against whatever it was. I've seen carnage, I've seen slaughter. This... this shit was something else. This was brutal."

"Jeez," Vincente breathed as he realized that Shannon really was afraid despite the rifle he carried.

"Let's get moving!" Hector shouted as he and Melts came hurrying out of the ship. Their rifles were up and scanning their surroundings.

"What about Kamol's list?" Vincente asked as the two men passed him where he stood.

"Forget it," Hector shook his head. "We need to get out of here. Now."

"But–"

"Now, Vincente."

Vincente nodded jerkily and jogged in the center of the squad of soldiers as they headed back for the Fancy. The planet's sky was beginning to darken and their shadows stretched out like giants across the sand. The lightning above was tapering off, and the air was becoming noticeably cooler. At a guess, Vincente would say that this was the planet's sunset. An ear-piercing cry that was utterly inhuman cut through the growing darkness of the planet's twilight.

"What in the devil was that?" Vincente asked Hector.

The leader of the mercenaries shook his head. "Hell if I know." He motioned with his hands and the others nodded. They fanned out in a protective formation, weapons at the ready.

Vincente's eyes scanned the desert around the group. There were several clusters of jagged rocks that whatever had made the sound might be hiding in or behind, but that was all he could see.

Hector and Vincente traded a look. Both of them knew they couldn't stay here but the masses of rocks offered ample cover for ambushes along their path. Vincente saw that the other mercenaries were uneasy as well. They were professionals and knew their business well enough to realize they were in danger.

"Shannon told me that something killed that ship's crew after it went down," Vincente commented, "and that there was no sign of the bodies."

Hector nodded. "If I were a gambling man, I'd wager it was some kind of indigenous predator or a pack of them. I'd also wager that we've just tipped them off to the fact that we're here... though I reckon the Fancy's own crash did that already."

"We're all armed," Vincente said, fingers going tighter around the butt of his pistol.

"So were the poor bastards on that ship from the look of things," Hector frowned, then spat into the sand. "I hate unknowns. Give me an enemy and at least I got a target to shoot at but spooky crap like this..."

"I hear you," Vincente said, then shrugged. "This is the sort of luck I have lived with my whole life. Sorry, if I didn't mention that earlier."

Vincente half-hearted joke got a chuckle out of Hector. "Maybe you should take point then. If whatever's out there comes after you first, the rest of us will have a chance to blow it to Hell."

"Said I was unlucky, not suicidal," Vincente responded.

"Right," Hector smiled. "That you did. Shannon, Jacob, you got the sharp end."

The shriek rang out a second time. It seemed to come from all around them, as if it were many voices mingled into a single cry. It set the nerves on edge and caused the men to grit their teeth. They picked up their pace and hurried to get back to the Fancy before whatever that was out there found them.

Vincente thought he was going to die by the time the Fancy finally came into sight. His body was slick with sweat and his breath came in ragged gasps that made his ribs hurt. His vision had become tunneled, focused solely on his ship and the hole in its hull that would allow them entry. Shannon and Jacob entered the ship first, turning back with their rifles aimed out into the sands, as the rest of the squad moved on inside past them.

Jasmine was waiting for them. The big mercenary, Yolo, was with at her side. Vincente dropped to the floor of the corridor like a stone in front of them. He looked up at Jasmine. "Next time, you get to be the one out there risking your butt."

"I want every opening in this ship's hull sealed off as best it can be!" Hector started barking orders. He whirled on Vincente who was still getting his breath back. "We're gonna need every able bodied hand on this, including that alien engineer of yours."

"Fine, whatever you need," Vincente croaked. "Wake me when it's over."

With that said, Vincente promptly passed out, sprawling out onto the floor.

****

"This place is fucking hell," a voice Vincente vaguely recognized as Yolo woke him from his slumber.

"How long was I out this time?" He found himself, once more, in the partially ruined med-bay. The auto-doc table where the grievously injured mercenary had been before was now empty. Nobody commented on this, so Vincente decided it was not time to press the issue.

Kamol and Jasmine were in the room with him. Yolo stood just outside the door, his bulk preventing him from seeing beyond. Jasmine stood just inside the door leading into the corridor, while Kamol paced nervously back and forth. The small Lorn swiveled his head and looked at Vincente with coal black eyes.

"Zoola," Kamol answered, contempt barely out of his tone.

"Ten hours?" Vincente sat up in horror. "Why didn't you wake me?"

"Given how hard you'd been hitting the stims, I figured you could use the sleep. Besides, other than Hector and his boys going all gung-ho at securing the ship, not much has happened. We're still stuck here, and we're still screwed," she finished.

"No sign of the..." Vincente paused. He didn't know what was out there, but he could hear the monstrous shriek of whatever it was inside his head.

"Not yet at any rate," Jasmine said, "Hector sure thinks it's coming, though."

"Chaden rooz, Vincente," Kamol added. He continued, saying that Hector hadn't been happy with the original attempts to secure the breaches in the hull. Kamol went on to explain that what power he had been able to restore to the ship's systems was now being channeled into its defensive screens. The skin sealant, which typically protected the interior of the ship from the vacuum of space was still down, though.

"That's not good," Vincente rose from his bed. His knees were shaky under him, but he found he could stand. "We're going to need that power if we do find a means to get the Fancy space-worthy again."

Kamol's head reared back in the guttural set of clicking noises that passed for laugher among his species. "Fula. Asa fula."

The alien was serious in spite of his flippant reply, but Vincente just couldn't admit that the Fancy was dead. Her loss hurt too much to deal with right now.

"The only real hope we have is finding another ship," Jasmine said. "There should be plenty for the taking if all the missing ships in the stories about this world crashed like we did. We just have to locate them. Can you fix the Aardvark?"

"Grob. Norfellen dou?" Kamol laughed again.

"Agreed," Jasmine moved closer to Kamol. "The mercs are spooked. Getting them to give up any shred of power for the Fancy's sensors, even if I can get them to work somehow with all the interference in the atmosphere, won't be easy. They're sure the devil himself is out there and just waiting on them to make a wrong move."

"I trust Hector's instincts," Vincente rubbed his unshaven cheeks. He really should have shaved before meeting Mooney. "The mercs are freaked out for a reason. I didn't go into that other ship with them but from how they tell it, whatever got that crew will be coming for us too. It's just a matter of time."

"Hector says that something marked inside," Yolo said as he poked his head inside the med-bay. "Like an animal marking its territory. We're in that territory, or crossed its border, I dunno."

"Territorial dominant predator," Vincente shook his head. "I should have hired some Wild Ones."

"They'd probably fall down and worship the damn thing, boss," Jasmine said. She tilted her head and smiled. "There's a reason they love me."

"All right. Suggestions?" Vincente asked.

"Getting the sensors online wouldn't just allow us to locate other ships close by, they might tell us what it is we're up against out there too," Jasmine said.

"Hector's gonna freak," Yolo predicted.

"Can we work some sort of compromise out?" Vincente asked. Yolo shrugged.

"You can try," the big man offered,

"Make them your first priority, Kamol," Vincente ordered. "In the meantime," he turned to Jasmine. "Let's go see if we can hammer some sense into our guests and help them see the light."

They moved forward in the downed ship, passing the mercenary berthing cabins and into the large open area. There they found Hector, along with Shannon and Melts, quietly discussing a defensive perimeter. Hector stopped and looked up as he saw Vincente up and out of bed.

"Enjoy your nap?" Hector asked in a nasty tone as Vincente approached him. The mercenaries had turned the exposed bay into a fortress, with old canisters and metallic containers blocking all of the damaged portions of the hull except for the largest hole. There, he had placed two large, belt-fed automatic machine guns to protect the entrance. Both were thermal guided and automated, which Vincente knew would shred anything that did not show up in the human body temperature range.

"Not really," Vincente said. He motioned around him. "You been busy."

"Georgie died," Hector announced without preamble. Vincente blinked, confused for a moment, until he remembered the wounded mercenary.

"I'm sorry."

Hector shook his head. "I actually can't blame you for this. Your auto-doc is top rate, especially for a tramp freighter. He just lost too much blood and had too many internal injuries to recover from."

"Where's... the body?" Vincente asked.

"Taken care of," was all Hector said. Vincente coughed slightly. He was embarrassed and ashamed at his own embarrassment. Mercenaries died all the time. It was why they were called soldiers of fortune, after all, he reasoned internally.

"Boss," Jasmine jogged him with an elbow. Vincente nodded.

"Look, we may have come up with an idea to get back to that ship and pilfer parts that we need," Vincente said, "as well as scanning the area to find the other ships, potentially."

"I thought we are in this mess because your scanners weren't working," Hector accused.

"The storms have died down, in case you've forgotten," Jasmine said.

"If we could just get a small portion of the power you're using for our shielding, we might be able to—"

"No."

"Excuse me?" Vincente looked at the mercenary, surprised. "This is my ship."

"And security is my job," Hector said firmly, though there was no heat in his tone. "You hired me because you wanted Ms. Mooney's best. I'm that. For now, that shield stays up."

"For how long?" Vincente wondered. "It'll be easier getting us out of here if we knew where the other ships were. We could scavenge food, ammo, who knows what else from them."

"He's right, boss," Yolo said with a grunt. "Sorta."

"How long are the nights here? Anybody know?" Hector asked. Seeing a collective negative shake of heads, he continued. "All right, I'll give some power for the scan once the night is over. Not a moment before then, though."

"That could be a while," Jasmine warned. "The rotation of the planet, and the degree that it's tilted on, could affect the length of the night. I can guess, but I might be off. Give me a bit and some pen and paper, and I'll give it a go."

"Then we all better get comfortable," Hector said. "We may be here awhile."

INTERLUDE III

"Please state your name for the record."

The fastidiously dressed man coughed and leaned forward, speaking directly into the microphone. "I am Professor Hans Jurgen, Ph.D."

"And what is your field of specialty?"

"I am an extraterrestrial ecologist and accredited instructor of exobiology at Old Oxford on Earth," the professor said, with just a touch of pride in his voice.

"Is it difficult to attain your position or expertise?"

"Of course!" the professor announced, shock and surprise etched deep into his tone. "Old Oxford isn't like that uppity Oxford on Europa, you know. Old Oxford is the original Oxford, dating back to 1096! You must be a master in your field, plus have the proper credentials, in addition to being connected to the right people, before you are even considered as an applicant for a teaching position. To become tenured, it takes twenty years of hard work and dedication, as well as be on the cutting edge of theoretical probabilities in post-modern exo-evolutionary xenobiology!"

The prosecutor pinched the bridge of his nose. "I'm sorry, doctor. I didn't grasp all that. What precisely does it all mean?"

"It means..." Professor Jurgen's voice trailed off for a moment as he struggled to answer. After a minute of thought, his shoulders slumped in defeat. "It means that you must be able to justify your funding by being a world-class bullshitter."

"But you're still the authority on exobiology, correct?" the prosecutor asked as he tapped a few notes onto his screen.

"What did you write down there?" The professor tried to lean across the table to see, but stopped as the prosecutor gave him an icy look. Jurgen meekly sat back down in his chair and began to fiddle with his tie. After another minute of awkward silence, he remembered that he had been asked a question. "Oh, yes. Yes, I am."

"So can you tell us in your professional opinion, what the planet coded as Gorgon IV is like?"

"From what we've theorized running computer models, the planet is luxurious in plant life, due to the massive greenhouse effect that pervades across the world," the professor began, warming up slowly to the lecture he had prepared days before. "Animal life should be diverse and exotic, akin to the way the Amazon was thousands of years before, unspoiled by the hand of man. There should be plenty of water, and though the atmosphere is turbulent, it is stable enough to support life. In fact, it could be theorized that, thanks to our computer models, Gorgon IV is the extraterrestrial version of our Eden."

"Your... computer models?"

"Yes," the professor sniffed. "The majority of my colleagues agree with my findings on the theoretical data. The planet should be a paradise."

"Perhaps you can enlighten me then," the prosecutor said as he looked back down at his screen. "Why is a paradise planet called Murder World?"

"There probably is some dangerous wildlife on a planet," the professor allowed. "Perhaps some super predator that has not had ten thousand years of learning to avoid man. Something big, strong, agile and fast. But I believe – and again, the majority of my colleagues agree with me – that the primary reason it earned that nickname was due to the unfortunate rumors which sprung up after the loss of the Gnarler. Her captain was a war hero, you know. Stopped the Zebulun incursion into our space. His ship was lost there, along with a few others, and suddenly rumor sprang up that the planet was like Earth's Bermuda Triangle. Superstitious mumble-jumble, if you ask me. Our models suggest–"

"I'm sorry to interrupt–" the prosecutor was not sorry "–but... what models?"

"Our highly advanced and technically sound computer models," the professor sniffed again. The prosecutor was growing tired of that particular trait. "We've run climate models, population control models, and water purification models on these computer simulations throughout the years. We can predict what is going to happen, and so we push for change to occur before we hit that tipping point. Governments listen to us and usually follow suit."

"So how often are your models correct?"

"Well, that's a variable number, because oftentimes the success rate is measured in whether or not a government listens to our suggestions and changes policy," the professor admitted. "It also means that, because most listen to us, that our model percentage rate of success is often low. But that doesn't mean we're wrong, really. It simply means that the changes we proposed are working. Empirical data suggests—"

"So then you're certain that Gorgon IV is a habitable, comfortable world with only a few predators to contend with?" the prosecutor interrupted again.

"Oh, certainly," the professor nodded eagerly. "I'd live there, if not for the lack of university for me to teach at. I'm not an ideal candidate to colonize a planet. I'm not a simple laborer. But... yes, our models suggest that the planet is a veritable paradise. An absolute pristine and perfect paradise."

CHAPTER SIX

"This place is a damned hell," Yolo groused as he looked out one of the smaller holes in the hull of the Fancy. It was completely black outside and he couldn't see more than ten feet. He shivered and pulled his jacket collar up. "It's either way too hot or too damned cold."

"You complain a lot," Jasmine countered, her feet propped up on a table in front of where she was sitting. She had been reading more about the schematics of the ship, and something was nagging at her. She wasn't sure what it was, but there was something buried in the information at hand which was wrong. "Back when I was in the Defense Corps, we spent four months on Shiva. You want cold? You could take a leak and it would be frozen before it hit the ground. For us girls, that meant getting our pants down, peeing, then getting them back up before your lady parts froze. All while not setting your rifle down, because the metal would freeze and damage the barrel. This? This is a heat wave compared to that."

"You were in the Corps?" Yolo asked, impressed. "That explains how easily you took me down."

"That, and the fact that you led with your left and telegraphed the motions of going for your gun," Jasmine explained. "You have bad balance. It was easy to keep you from getting centered."

"Are you single?" he asked as Vincente strode into the bay. Jasmine chuckled and stood up, schematics in hand.

"Got any ideas?" Vincente asked.

She shook her head. "Nothing so far. It looks like we'll have the scavenge parts off of the other ship, if we can get back to it. We might be able to look for some others if the interference from the atmosphere wasn't so bad."

"Can't," Vincente said. "We're still using the extra power for the sensors to reinforce the shielding. As long as we have no visual out there, Hector doesn't want to risk whatever happened to that other ship happening to us. I'm inclined to agree with him."

"Well, we won't finish the job if we don't find that research vessel of theirs," Jasmine needlessly reminded him. "Plus, I keep looking over our schematics and something just seems off..."

"Nice setup you guys have here," he said as he pointed a finger at the two machine guns set up at the entrance of the largest tear. "Those fully automated?"

"Yep," Jasmine smiled, the pride in her work showing. "Yolo may be a dunce otherwise, but he knows his guns. We set up an infrared scanner to look out and linked it to the firing mechanism of the guns, so anything that pops up within fifty yards gets a rude surprise. Jacob and Melts are over on the other side, but their gap isn't as big as this one. So we've doubled up on the defenses here, and they're got the infrared goggles over there and rifles. All's quiet, though. Plus, Shannon's coming on in a few to relieve Yolo, so the big baby can get in his comfy bed and stay warm."

"Any problems?" he asked, pointing his chin towards Yolo. Jasmine shook her head.

"Nope. He's been a good boy. Only had to threaten him once, so far."

"Good," Vincente grunted. "I'm going to run down and talk to Kamol. I have an idea, but I want to run it past him first to see if it's feasible."

"What do you want me to do in the meantime?" Jasmine asked.

"Try not to kill anyone?" he suggested as he walked out of the bay. He passed through the mercenary berthing area and slid down the small ladder, which led to engineering. The deeper into the bowels of the ship he went, the odder the decor became. He had known that the Lorn had decorated his space to remind him of his home world, though he doubted that snow globes of Earth were culturally significant on the little alien's world. Still, who was he to judge? He had a bobble-head hula girl stuck on the copilot's dash up in the cockpit.

"Kamol?" Vincente called out as he knocked on the closed door to the engine room.

"Dou?"

"I've got a couple questions. You got a moment?"

"Shazu. Para coomt."

Vincente pushed the door open and entered the dimly lit area. The small alien was seated at a workbench, a tool in his hand that Vincente didn't recognize. He was working on a scanner of some sort. Vincente could tell, but other than that, how the alien kept the ship up in the sky was sometimes beyond him. He typically left the Lorn to his own devices, and miracles happened. He closed the door behind him.

"I've got an idea that I want to run past you," Vincente said. "Do you think we could run the scanners still while keeping the shielding up?"

"Tsin... varks panta dou?"

"Yeah, I didn't think so, but I wanted to check."

"Corga vacha. Bila cun darsh et, sin."

"Wait. What do you mean, half power?"

"Shazu. Dona et."

"Up to four quadrants, huh," Vincente pursed his lips, his expression thoughtful as his mind went over the theory. "You know that Hector won't let me drop shielding unless it's clear, right? It might not be enough time to scan more than one or two quadrants."

"Chinzahaduum."

"Oh, thanks a lot, pal," Vincente groused. "It'll be your problem as well if we don't get off the ground. Well, I'm going to try and talk Hector into letting us try it out. Plus, I want you to get down to the starboard cargo hold and put the Aardvark together. I'm not walking in that heat again, I don't care what anybody thinks. You be ready for the call on the shields as well, okay?"

"Shazu."

Vincente popped the door back open and came face to face with Hector. The mercenary leader was scowling, which the captain had learned was never a good thing. He softly shut the door to Kamol's space before he met Hector's gaze.

"Shouldn't be down here, Hector," Vincente reminded him. "Kamol's territorial, and we saw what happened the last time someone messed with his stuff."

"That was more of a disagreement of styles," Hector reminded him. "There's some weird noises outside. Like... I don't know, maybe some kind of mating cry? It's hard to tell."

"So you think whatever hit that downed freighter out there is out there now?"

"Without a doubt, something is out there," Hector said. "I talked with Jasmine, and she told me that she wants to scan for that downed military ship. I'm vetoing it now."

"I figured you would. So I talked to Kamol, and he came up with a better plan. Well, more of a suggestion, really."

"Yeah, I still want to kick your teeth in," Hector admitted. "Ms. Mooney said I'd want to kick your teeth in every time you said something."

"Kamol thinks that he can keep the shielding up and use some of the power to do a quadrant search for the research vessel," Vincente explained, ignoring Hector's reference to his wife. "Not a big one, but we can eliminate at least one area, maybe two."

"As long as we don't have sensors to scan the immediate area, no," Hector said. "I'm not compromising ship security just so you can make a quick credit."

"You won't get paid, either," Vincente said, annoyed.

"Dead men only vote. They don't get to spend their money," Hector said with finality and climbed back up the ladder. Vincente frowned. Behind him, Kamol's door opened. The alien looked at him questioningly.

"You got the sensors set up and ready?" he asked. The alien nodded. "Okay, good. Go put the Aardvark together. I'll get it through Hector's thick head that this is important."

"Thana dou?"

"I have no idea how," Vincente said. "I'd have an easier time getting Mooney to forgive me. Just get the Aardvark ready, will you?"

"Shazu."

He clambered up the ladder after Hector. They needed to find another ship to salvage parts from, and the military ship was probably the best one for that in terms of parts. He doubted they'd find a lot of edible supplies, though, but they had enough food and water for another two weeks before they would start to run into trouble.

He found Hector back in the cargo bay with Jasmine, Yolo and Shannon. They were heatedly discussing the possibility of searching for any downed ship, with Hector adamant about not going out until it was lighter and they could see more. Vincente walked in just at the tail end of the argument.

"Look, I'm keeping us alive," Hector said. "We need to make it through the night. Then we can discuss possibilities."

"We don't know how long these nights last!" Jasmine protested loudly.

"She's right," Vincente said. "Time is not on our side here. We need to seize the initiative and do that search now, or else we won't have enough time to find something and get out there to check it out."

"Not happening, captain," Hector said. "We already had this discussion. As long as it's too dark to see, we're not venturing out."

"The sensors might be able to punch through the atmospheric interference now, before those weird plasma storms start back up!" Vincente said, his voice rising. "When it's daylight out, the storms may be too strong."

"And until it gets lighter out, I say no. End of story," Hector said and crossed his arms emphatically. Vincente rolled his eyes.

"Damn it!" he exploded. "We need to do this now!"

"No, we don't."

"Yes, we do!"

"Is it me," Jasmine interrupted the arguing men. "Or is the sky getting lighter?"

Both men glanced towards the large hole in the hull. Sure enough, the blackness was subtly shifting to a light grey. They still could not see beyond the ship very far, but dawn couldn't be too far away. Vincente and Hector looked at one another, their argument forgotten.

"You said that the lightning in the clouds was interfering with the sensors before we crashed," Hector said to Jasmine, his voice excited and the quarrel momentarily forgotten. "Have the bolts started up again?"

"No," Jasmine said after a quick check. "Not yet. Just a normal sunrise. Well, as normal as this planet can get."

"Okay, captain" Hector nodded, caving at last. "Go ahead with your cockamamie scheme."

Vincente did not waste any time. He flicked on the comm. "Kamol, drop the power to the shields by half. Jasmine, get in the cockpit, bring up the scanners, and create a search pattern. Expand it as far as you can, then do a grid-by-grid search. Look for protruding metal, emergency beacons, power sources, stuff like that."

"Shazu."

"On it."

"I sure hope this works, Vincente," Hector said as Jasmine pushed past him.

"Me too," the captain nodded. "It's a risk, but a calculated one. In fact, since the night was–"

Both automated machineguns exploded into action simultaneously, empty shell casings bouncing around on the steel floor as thousands of rounds suddenly poured out the opening they were protecting. Everyone jumped, and the mercenaries pulled their rifles up and to their shoulders. Vincente grabbed his pistol, though he was not sure what to do with it.

Outside, something primal and dark screamed. The cry cut straight to the soul, causing the fine hairs on the back of everyone's neck to stand. It was an ancient fear, one that they shouldn't have recognized. A small part of the brain did, though, and they all knew it. The automated guns suddenly quit firing. Silence, except for the collective ringing in their ears, fell over the ship once more. The mercenaries moved closer to the machineguns and looked outside.

"Clear right," Shannon said, his body pressed against the hull.

"Clear left," Yolo said.

"All clear," Hector said. The mercenaries lowered their rifles as their leader turned and looked at Vincente. He pointed outside. "Whatever the hell that is, captain, it's smart. It's testing us, testing our defenses. It's patient and it's waiting."

"Then we better find those downed ships," Vincente said. "And fast."

"Got a ping!" Jasmine yelled over the comm. "Fifteen miles off to the magnetic west, southwest maybe. Getting coordinates now."

"Finally, some good news," Vincente breathed.

"Fifteen miles? You about croaked yesterday when we walked to that nearby ship," Shannon laughed. "Your fat ass is gonna die this time."

Vincente smirked. He switched comms. "Kamol, you got the Aardvark up and running yet?"

"Shazu," came the immediate reply.

"What the hell is an aardvark?"

"Really?" Vincente mocked the mercenary. "What line of business are you in again?"

Hector scowled at him, waiting on a real answer.

"It's an eight man APC," Jasmine explained. "The good captain here won one in a game of cards a while back. Without cheating, I'll add. We've been toting the thing around in one of the bays ever since. Damn thing takes up more room than it's worth."

"But I bet you're glad we have now," Vincente said.

"Shareel kappla dou?" Kamol started up again, concern evident in his voice.

"I'm sure it'll be fine, Kamol," Vincente blew off the small alien's warning that the APC wasn't one hundred percent functional at the moment. "You have two hours to finish getting it ready."

"Paka dou? Ohn merde shazu!" Kamol cursed again and headed off at a hurried pace.

"Was that in French?" Melts asked, confused. "He speaks French now?"

"Beats the heck out of walking, if your engineer can get it up to speed," Hector admitted after a moment. "With that thing out there, I was seriously questioning our ability to leave the ship at all, much less hoof it fifteen miles. Is this Aardvark of yours armed?"

Vincente nodded. "One anti-personnel canon mounted on a roof turret. Forty mike-mike rounds. Anti-material rounds, truc, but it should be more than enough to handle whatever's out there."

"Nice," Hector commented. "That'll make things a lot safer too."

"Jasmine, download the coordinates of that ship to the Aardvark's Navcomp. We'll roll out as soon as everybody's ready."

****

The Fancy could not be left unmanned, so Jasmine, Yolo, and Kamol stayed behind while Vincente, Hector, Melts, Jacob, and Shannon headed out in the Aardvark. The APC's steering system was pretty standard so Melts, after a quick crash course from Kamol, got stuck behind the wheel. Vincente and Hector sat in the vehicle's forward section with Melts, using the individual gun ports to help provide protection.

The Fancy's bay doors opened to allow it to exit. Testing the engine and finding it satisfactory, Melts nodded. The APC lurched out onto the sands of Gorgon IV, the heavy vehicle bouncing on the ground as it left the launch ramp. True daylight had yet to arrive, despite the extra time Kamol had spent working to get the Aardvark up and running. The overhead cloud cover was lighter than the previous day, with merely a thin layer of cover. The lightning was gone as well, allowing them to see the first hints of the massive sun that Gorgon IV orbited. The sky was purple and orange as the planet's sun began to slowly creep over the horizon, dawn rapidly approaching.

Jasmine had allowed them fifteen minutes to reach the other ship, two hours to check it out and salvage anything useful, and another fifteen minutes for their return trip. She had allotted extra time for the trip, but still was cutting it close. Ten miles was still too far in Gorgon IV's mess of an atmosphere. With all its interference, for them to count on the comm channels working would be foolish. The established time table would help those staying behind know if something was up, though she had admitted that she wasn't quite sure what help they could be if something did happen.

Once the APC was clear of the Fancy, Melts kicked it into high gear. The vehicle's max speed was close to sixty miles per hour, even with the heavy body armor surrounding the already-sturdy frame. The massive 454 cubic inch, V-10 Kesenault twin-turbocharged engine roared loudly as Melts pushed the vehicle to its limits. The huge wheels spun, throwing up sand as it picked up speed. Melts steered the Aardvark westward.

"The sensors on this thing are as screwed as the ship's," Melts complained as he drove. His eyes moved back and forth between the digital display and the windshield. "I mean, I'm not even picking up the Fancy right now, and it's right behind us."

"Nothing's perfect," Vincente sighed. He had figured this may happen. "Guess we'll have to play this old school. Can you handle it?"

Melts chuckled darkly. "Are you asking if I can read a map?"

One of Vincente's eyebrows arched up.

"Yeah, I can get us there, no worries," Melts assured them. "We don't need anything fancy to get us there, especially with the Navcomp coordinates already plugged in. The land here is so flat that it's hard to imagine anyone could get lost. Besides, getting a visual on something the size of that ship Jasmine located should be a walk in the park."

The windshield was the APC's only large viewing port on the vehicle. The rest of its body was pure armor, except for the gun turret on the top. Keeping an eye out for whatever was stalking them was going to be the hardest part of the trip, unless it happened to stumble out right in front of them. Since everyone on board knew that the odds of that happening were lower than them getting off the planet alive, someone was going to have to ride up in the gun turret. Vincente knew there was no way in stone cold Hades that it was going to be him. He was the captain and crap rolled downhill. He shot a glance at Hector, who nodded. The mercenary had been thinking the same exact thing.

"Jacob?" Hector looked at his subordinate.

"Yeah?"

"Up top."

"What? Why me?"

"Because me Boss, you piss ant. Get up there."

Though long-range comm systems were practically useless, Jasmine and Kamol had been able keep the localized ones operating through the planet's interference. They had rigged the comms up in the Aardvark to be able to punch through the overall interference, if in a small radius around the APC. That meant Jacob could talk to them through his helmet from the turret and maintain some sort of lookout, as well keep up comms for up to forty feet. Theoretically.

As the crashed ship came into view, there was no mistaking the lean, aggressive lines of a military ship. Vincente knew that it had to be the ship that they had been sent after. Though designated a research vessel, its military origin was unmistakable in the design of its hull. The additional armament atop the hull, as well as the missile ports, practically screamed military.

Melts brought the Aardvark to a halt a few hundred yards away from the ship and felt the turret above rotate as Jacob looked around for any signs of trouble. Once he received the all clear, he slowly brought the APC closer to the vessel.

It was much smaller than Vincente expected. He had guessed it would be more like a freighter, but the ship appeared more to be some sort of armed courier. He easily recognized the remnants of broken and smashed senor and weapons array spotted around and on the exterior of its hull. However, the reason that had caused the technologically advanced ship to come down in the first place wasn't evident.

"Well, there she is," Vincente said to no one in particular. "Any sign of our friend out there?"

"Negative," Jacob reported from the APC's turret. "All clear."

Vincente turned to Hector. "I reckon this is the point where you take over."

"Right," Hector released the safety straps of his seat and stood, his shoulders hunched in the cramped cabin. He tapped his helmet twice and grunted. "Melts, keep the engine hot. If I come running out of there, I don't want the engine to have problems turning over or anything stupid. Jacob, keep on the over watch. Shoot anything that looks dangerous. In fact, I want you to shoot it even if it doesn't. Shannon, you're with me." Hector started for the Aardvark's side door and paused, looking back at Vincente. "You coming?"

"To be honest, I'd rather sit this one out," Vincente shrugged, and then started releasing his own safety straps. He checked his holster for his handgun and nodded. "But yeah, I guess I am."

Shannon took point, the thin man leading them out of the APC and into the morning light. Vincente, following him out, blinked as he stepped out of the APC and the harsh rays of the sun hit his eyes. He raised a hand to shield his eyes and followed. Hector brought up the rear, turning back occasionally to ensure that nothing was trying to sneak up on them from near the APC.

"Ya know, I kind of thought it would be bigger," Vincente admitted as he stared at the ship in front of them.

"I'm not complaining," Hector said, moving to stand at his side. "A ship like that has a crew of... what, six?"

"Three, maybe four," Vincente corrected as they continued towards it. "It's highly unlikely we'll find much in the way of supplies on it. See the curves of its forward section? That sucker is built for hard speed and long travel. Its crew would most likely be in grav couches and possibly stasis for most of its travel time. We might get lucky on some of the parts Kamol needs, though. Military ships of its kind are all about redundant systems, so odds are that not everything was destroyed in the crash."

"Good to know," Hector grunted. "Now, how to do we get inside it?"

Unlike the Fancy or the other ship they had found after their arrival, this ship's hull appeared entirely intact. Its armor was badly mauled, even melted, in some places but there were no clear breaches in its hull. Vincente frowned and looked around, but couldn't see any sign of an entry point.

"Over here!" Shannon called. He had moved on to inspect the ship's exterior from its other side while the two other men were still talking. "There's an airlock on this side."

Vincente noticed that Hector kept worriedly glancing around for any sign of the predator that had dragged away the ship's crew. There was always the possibility that it could be lingering, staling them. The three men clustered in front of the airlock, eager to be inside where it would be presumably safer. Shannon's fingers played over its controls, which beeped warningly at him. The mercenary swore softly and tried again. Something in the frame gave a clicking noise. The airlock dilated open before them.

"Power's still on in there," Shannon said, stating the obvious. Vincente began to wonder whether that was a good thing.

"After you," Vincente motioned for Hector to enter the ship. He knew who should take the lead when it came to exploring a mysteriously crashed ship, and an out-of-shape man was not it. Hector grunted and moved in.

Vincente and Shannon followed.

****

Melts sat in the Aardvark's driver seat, impatiently rapping the tips of his fingers against the dashboard as a means of release for some of the nervous energy that threatened to overwhelm him. His eyes continually flicked across the horizon, looking for any sign of danger or life. He almost wished he had gone out with the others, instead of being stuck in the idling vehicle waiting for them to return. At least they had something to do.

It took twenty mind-numbing minutes before one of them finally broke radio silence.

"You bored yet?" Jacob asked over the comm. Melts was grateful for the break in routine, though he was mildly worried about annoying the captain of the Fancy. Ms. Mooney, despite her obvious dislike of the man, still held him in some esteem, though he wasn't sure why.

"You know it," Melts responded. "How's the view?"

"Nothin' to write home about," Jacob said. Melts felt movement from above as the turret swiveled. "Yep. Still nothin'. Lots of sand. Lots of rock. This place sucks."

"What glory is there in a common good," Melts quoted, thinking upon the works of Marlowe once more to ease the boredom, "if the common good drives me insane because there's nothing to do?"

"Huh?" Jacob asked over the comm. Melts shook his head and sighed.

"Philistine."

"I wonder why the Zebulun never claimed this planet as their own," Jacob muttered. "It's close enough to their space that they could take it and nobody would even say a word." The vehicle rocked again. Melts frowned.

"Rotating the turret won't make the time pass faster, Jacob."

"That wasn't me," Jacob said. Melts realized that he was right.

"How's the wind?"

"Not too bad," Jacob answered. The turret swiveled. "Yeah, hardly any at all actually. Weird."

The APC rocked again. "

"What the frag was that?" Jacob cried out.

"Contact?" Melts asked.

"I don't– frag me! Contact! Contact!"

Melts leaned forward in his seat, peering out the window. He couldn't see anything from his point of view except the endless sands and jagged outcropping of rocks which littered the immediate surface of Gorgon IV. Waves of heat shimmered from where the filtered rays of the planet's sun cooked the ground through the clouds, but that was all.

He started to ask if Jacob was all right when he heard the Aardvark's machine gun open up. A stream of high velocity rounds flashed above the window, every fifth round a tracer round. Melts cursed as his chin collided with the dash. He'd ducked for cover out of instinct, and had damn near broken his jaw in the process. Rubbing his cheek, he peeked back up over the dash. There was nothing that he could see out the window.

"Jacob, what's up there?"

Jacob was still firing. Melts could hear the clinging noises of spent shell cases pinging off the Aardvark's roof even through the sound of the gun's continuous fire. Oddly, he could hear little else. The sneaking suspicion that Jacob couldn't hear him over the continuous gunfire tickled the back of his mind.

Melts drew his sidearm and checked the chamber. A round was loaded and ready. He growled at his own lack of readiness, though he had a decent enough reason. His rifle was tucked away in the APC's rear compartment with the rest of his gear, since the driver's chair was no place for any equipment to be stored.

He looked down and tried to play with the sensor, but they were going wonky. One second, they showed hundred of thousands of contacts. The next, there was one. He tried flipping through the different frequencies to try to burn through the interference. He had no luck. Without functional sensors, he was effectively blind beyond what he could see through the window. That, he realized, was not a winning proposition.

"What the hell's going on out there?" Melts yelled over the comm. "Jacob? Acknowledge your comm, damn it!"

"Hostile contact!" Jacob howled back at him. "I got movement everywhere, and it ain't friendly!"

"Visual?"

"Negative!"

"Then how the hell–"

"Weapons hot!" Jacob practically screamed. "Get the boss on the horn!"

Melts tried, even though he knew better, to raise Hector over the comm. The atmospheric conditions were blocking them, and they still had one hundred minutes or so, before they were due back to the Aardvark. He received only the crackle of a broken channel for his efforts, and though he was dismayed, he had known the probable outcome of his efforts.

He had to help Jacob, but he wasn't sure how. There was no way in Hell he was about to open the side door of the APC without knowing what, precisely, the current threat was. Melts felt helpless as he continued to stare at nothing except sand out the window. The turret was constantly moving, he could tell that much at least. Jacob had the thing rotating in a three hundred and sixty degree arc, firing on full auto. Either the man had lost it, or they were massively FUBARed.

"How many targets?" Melts yelled over the comm to Jacob. His friend did not reply. "Stay with me, Jacob. C'mon man, how many targets!"

Jacob's answer was a fear-induced battle cry, followed by screams of pain. Melts was already moving towards the turret hatch in the back of the APC when what was left of Jacob tumbled from it. Blood splashed over Melts and the interior walls of the Aardvark as Jacob's corpse struck the floor in front of him. The man's entire upper body was gone.

With the gun silent, Melts could hear a strange, echoing shriek outside. A black-scaled hand reached downward through the open hatch, impossibly long fingers clawing at the air. Whether it was after the remains of Jacob or a new victim, Melts didn't know and didn't care. He jerked the barrel of his pistol up towards it and put two rounds into the arm above its wrist. The thing it belonged to made a pained, hissing noise like something between the cry of an injured cat and something far more reptilian in nature. The hand withdrew rapidly. Melts rushed forward, firing wildly upwards through the hatch. He heard a scuffling sound as whatever was up there backed away. Without wasting a second, he slammed the hatch shut and locked it in place. The thing above him returned, scratching at the hatch's cover with a sound like fingernails raking down an old-fashioned blackboard.

Darting back to the driver's compartment, Melts threw himself into the seat at the Aardvark's controls. His fingers stabbed at the console, activating the blast shield that slid into place over the vehicle's sole window. When the blast shield sunk into place, Melts slumped in his chair. His nerves were a mess. The knuckles of his right hand were white from the pressure his fingers exerted on the butt of his pistol as he clung to it as if a lifeline, holding it ready. The whole APC swayed and shook as something massive and heavy crashed against the side, trying to force its way inside.

Melts heard a soft whispering from nearby and realized that he was the source. Not a religious man since he moved away from home years before, he found himself whispering the Lord's Prayer under his breath, the barrel of his sidearm pressed against his forehead. As suddenly as it all started, it ended. Silence fell around him once more. His hands trembling, Melts sat his pistol on the dash and ran his hands through his hair. What the Hell am I supposed to do now? he wondered. There was no hope of reaching Hector and the others over the comm to warn them, and though they'd be able to see the Aardvark fully armored and the mess from Jacob on top, they wouldn't see anything at all unless they emerged from the other ship. By then, it would likely be too late. Whatever got Jacob would easily tear them apart.

He sat back in the chair. He couldn't leave Hector and the others, but he had to think of a way to warn them that they were under attack. He closed his eyes to think, and tried to put the ghastly image of Jacob's lower half resting in the back area aside.

CHAPTER SEVEN

Jasmine frowned as she looked over the readings. The radical tilt of the planet swung the magnetic north and south poles to almost seventy degrees away from where one would typically find them. This created, the computer surmised, an ion-charged atmosphere with varying polarities in their static charge. As a result, the electromagnetic storms, which filled the atmosphere, were typically larger than most landmasses of Earth.

She snorted, unimpressed. "Computer, you are flat-out wrong. Science doesn't work that way."

She leaned back in her pilot's chair and grabbed a digital reader. She pored over the ship schematics once more. Something was wrong, but she was still unable to put her finger on it. The skin around the hull, which would have sealed any and all punctures to prevent a complete and violent decompression in space, was still not sealing the holes which had been caused during the crash. It was unheard of for the skin not to work, and she was determined to figure out just what was going on.

She swiveled in the chair and began to input more numbers into the system. A few seconds of computation later, a solution appeared. She frowned and she looked over the mathematics.

"Nope," she muttered. "Go home, computer, you're drunk."

"Hey," Yolo knocked on the door to the cockpit. "Busy?"

"Yeah," she said, "but you can come in. The computer is being stupid."

"My momma used to say that computers are only as smart as the people who use them," he said as he shifted his bulk into the co-pilot's chair, which was usually occupied by Vincente.

"So you're telling me I'm stupid?"

"No! Is that how it came out? Oh, God, please don't hurt me," Yolo said, his voice panicky as he held up his hands. Jasmine smiled thinly.

"I'm giving you crap, merc," she said. "Relax."

"Oh, okay," Yolo breathed a sigh of relief. He motioned at the computer. "So why is the computer being stupid?"

"It's suggesting that the atmosphere isn't the proper mixture of nitrogen and oxygen to keep the hull skin functioning," she explained, "which is stupid, because when we're in space, there's no oxygen or nitrogen to keep it working at all like the computer insists is needed."

"That is weird," Yolo nodded.

"That's not even the worst part," Jasmine said, warming up to her rant. "The schematics of the ship are off. That crash shouldn't have even scratched the paint, but it tore large chunks from the hull. We were hit by a missile once out– well, never mind where. But this old tub can take a beating, so the crash shouldn't have done the damage it did."

"What does the computer say?" Yolo asked.

"Data inconclusive," she snorted. "It thinks we collided with another ship in the atmosphere and crashed. I would have noticed another ship out there when we were coming in. No, something else is going on."

"Well, it's not like we could have seen something while coming in," Yolo suggested, playing Devil's Advocate for a moment. "You said we were blind earlier."

"Did we come to an abrupt halt?" she asked him. "Is there metal from another ship embedded in our hull?"

"Uh, no," he admitted.

"Our momentum would have drastically changed if we'd hit another ship," Jasmine said. "Physics can't be broken. Not like that, at least. An object in motion..."

"Okay, so maybe we hit a meteorite?" Yolo tried. Jasmine shook her head.

"Again, there'd be scorch marks, residue of damage, something," she explained. "No, the punctures are clean, curved inwards, and along both sides of the ship running almost straight up and down. It's... just weird."

"Hey, is that the Aardvark?" Yolo asked and pointed out at the distance. Jasmine squinted her eyes and spotted the tell-tale shape of the burly APC. She checked the clock and frowned.

"They're back an hour early," she said. "Get back there. Something went wrong."

Together, the two of them raced down into the starboard side cargo bay. Yolo grabbed his rifle and rested against the bulkhead next to the lever. Jasmine grabbed the lever and prepared to lower it.

"Visual?" she asked.

"Clear," Yolo responded. "APC is six hundred yards out and closing fast."

"Lowering bay door."

The large, heavy door began to lower, creating a ramp for the APC to ride in on. Yolo stuck his head out the opening and glanced around before tucking back in. He gave her a thumbs up.

"Two hundred yards!" he called out. Jasmine readied the lever. She wanted that door up as soon as they were inside.

A terrible cry erupted from the outside. Yolo's face turned white and he looked back out the cargo bay opening. He pressed his back against the cool metal.

"Clear! Arriving now!"

The APC rumbled up onto the metal deck and nearly slammed into the far wall. The entry brake, which was nothing more than a hydraulic lever with a large pad on it to slow them down, prevented them from crashing through the ship and destroying it more than it already was.

She flipped the lever and watched as the bay door began to rise. Another scream erupted from just outside. Yolo fired off a warning shot through the gap, but backed away as soon as he could. Yolo crouched near the APC, standing watch. His rifle was up and ready, pointed at the now-closed cargo bay door.

The back door of the APC opened and Shannon came out of the APC first, the small, bird-like man pale and terrified. Hector and Vincente followed next, with Melts bringing up the rear. Melts puked as soon as he was out of the APC, which both angered and worried Jasmine.

"Boss, what's wrong?" Jasmine asked, her hand resting the butt of her pistol. Yolo crouched near the APC, standing watch. His rifle was up and ready, pointed at the now closed cargo bay door. She did a mental count of everyone as they tumbled out of the APC and came up one short. "We're missing one. Where's Jacob?"

Vincente fell to his hands and knees and began to retch, his empty stomach heaving painfully as stomach bile spilled onto the deck. Drool and spittle dangling from his lower lip, he looked up and into the eyes of his pilot. They were filled with despair and terror. He slowly dragged himself off the floor and fell into one of the extra seats in the cargo bay. He accepted a small drink of water from Hector, whose expression was almost identical.

"We're all going to die," he said. "We're all going to die on this fucking planet, and they knew. They knew! Those goddamned cowards knew, and they sent us anyway!"

"Whoa, slow down, boss," Jasmine said as she grabbed a canteen that was filled with water. "What happened out there?" She passed it to Vincente, who greedily accepted it. He took a sip of water before he began to recount just what had happened inside the downed military vessel.

****

After Shannon managed to crack open the airlock, Hector took point, followed closely by Vincente. Shannon closed the airlock and sealed it, ensuring that nothing could sneak up on them from the outside. Once their eyes adjusted to the dim blue emergency lighting in the ship they began to explore, looking for any sign of the crew, replacement parts to fix the Fancy, or the precious databanks that they'd been hired to find.

Vincente and Hector decided to attempt to find some of the parts on the list Kamol had made for them. It was decidedly long, but Vincente figured that they had an even chance at finding about half of the items necessary to get his bird back into the sky. In the meantime, Shannon plugged into the vessel's databanks and began a hard-line download of its contents to the handheld unit he carried. He'd have to plug it into another computer to actually read it, but this way allowed him to download the immense databanks at three times the normal speed.

Aft of the airlock, Vincente followed Hector into the cramped space of the ship's main engineering section. He was sweating profusely, despite the short walk from the Aardvark to the downed ship, and he couldn't shake the feeling that they were being watched. His eyes tracked back and forth across the narrow passageway but there was no sign of the crew. Unlike the first ship they boarded, not even a clue as to what happened to the crew remained to be found. He tugged on his collar and readjusted the uncomfortable body armor. He hoped it was just his nerves messing with him and nothing more. He pulled out his sidearm at a signal from Hector and pushed up against the wall. Hector held up three fingers and pointed at the dogged lever. Vincente nodded and pointed his gun at the door. Hector quickly counted down and jerked the door open. He moved quickly out of Vincente's line of fire and the captain moved forward. He stepped inside and immediately moved to his right, clearing the small engineering space. Hector came right behind him, sweeping to the far corner.

"Clear," Hector murmured. Vincente nodded and holstered his firearm.

As Vincente took a glance at the ship's primary drive system, he whistled. It was top of the line and pure military grade, which he expected. What he hadn't thought he would see was the fact that the engine had a small, secondary system running throughout. He wasn't sure what it was for, but it was a backup to the backup. He already knew that the little ship could fly circles around the Fancy. He didn't even want make an educated guess at its top speed. The further he explored, the more he became confused by the redundancy of the system.

Just as odd as the sheer amount of power the drive could generate was the fact that not all the power was routed to propulsion and shields. Upon closer inspection, he saw a second set of conduits that ran power to another area of the ship. He muttered darkly at the abject stupidity of the military.

"What were you boys doing out here?" he asked the walls, which obviously did not answer. "You shouldn't need this much power. Not for what you said you were doing."

"What is it?" Hector had asked as Vincente moved to the single console and activated the ship's computer system. He typed in a few commands before he accessed the root command-sequencing page. Finding the right line sequence, he went to the main screen and began to dog around in the tech details of the ship. Finding what he wanted, he pointed.

"You tell me," Vincente said as the two of them stared at the screen.

It looked like a good portion of the power from the drive was diverted to a holding cell of some kind in the center of the ship. It was large, almost forty feet in all directions, with a reinforced Durasteel casing around the powered shielding. Hector took scratched at his forehead, nudging his helmet upwards to do so.

"You think they were carrying a Zebulun prisoner? Or a bunch of them?"

"Don't have a clue," Vincente admitted. "This ship is designed like a courier, not a prisoner transport. But this... cage suggests prisoner transport. Whatever they had in there, they sure seemed to have planned to get it wherever it was bound for as fast as they could."

Their comm clicked twice. Hector cocked his head sideways. "It's Shannon," he explained to Vincente. "Go ahead, Shannon."

"We need to get the hell out of here, right now," the other mercenary said. "I've found something that... I don't think I was meant to find. I'm logging it onto my datapad now to go over the information more thoroughly, but if this is what I think I saw while doing the hard download..."

"On our way," Hector cut off the comm. "C'mon captain, time to get off this ship."

"We'll need to come back for parts," Vincente reminded him. "Out in the open. Again."

"Cross that bridge when we come to it," the mercenary captain said as they stepped out of the engineering space. Vincente dogged the hatch behind them, just in case, and they hurried back towards the airlock, where they found Shannon waiting for them. The small man shoved a datapad into Vincente's hands.

"Take a look at that," Shannon barked at them.

Vincente's eyes scanned over the data. His eyes widened. "Impossible. Nobody's that stupid."

"That's what I thought as well," Shannon nodded. "Read the notes."

Vincente dragged his fingers across the screen and brought up the footnotes buried at the bottom of the page. The font grew larger and he began to read. After a moment, he nodded and swore softly. "That makes a hell of a lot of sense. Those bastards."

"What?" Hector demanded, growing impatient.

"Well, we're all going to die here," Vincente said and suddenly giggled like a mad man. "Didn't I tell you about my luck?"

Hector stared at Vincente as Shannon spoke up. "Boss, this is some hard-core crap, man. This vessel wasn't here to spy on the Zebulun, and it sure as Hades wasn't a research vessel either. The crew of this ship was sent here to collect a life form from Gorgon IV and bring it home."

"What kind of life form?"

"They were calling it 'Specimen X'. But... easier to explain it this way, from the notes. You ever heard the word Kaiju?" Vincente asked.

Hector shook his head.

"It's an old Earth word, Japanese in origin that means something close to strange creature or monster. According to this, Gorgon IV is home to a group of beings, for lack of a better word that fit that description. Whatever these things are, they're far more than that. It says here that the Zebulun think of them as gods, or at least some sort of terrible demons. There are seven of them in all and each one of them is a pretty nasty mother. The plan was to capture one, preferably a small one, for study and see if the thing could be weaponized in a potential war with the Zebulun. Or anybody else, for that matter."

"And they had one on this ship." Hector concluded.

Shannon nodded. "That's not the worst part though. . ."

Vincente tapped the screen of the console he and Hector had been examining, "All that extra power that was being fed to our mysterious holding cell... it's offline. So much for redundancy, eh?"

"Oh crap," Hector said as he got it. He jerked his rifle up into a ready position.

"Um. . .and there's not just seven," Shannon added in. "The seven described in the ship's logs are only the, hmm... hive leaders?"

A soft, subtle clacking sound came from nearby. Vincente jerked his sidearm back from the holster. Shannon pocketed the datapad and a small carbine appeared in his hands as if by magic. He crouched and began to sweep across the passageway.

"Clear," Shannon murmured.

"Contact!" Hector suddenly shouted. All three of them looked up as something black and fast slithered across the ceiling above them. Whatever it was, it moved too fast to get a good look at. Hector opened up, firing in controlled bursts in the direction that the creature had moved. Small caliber rounds tore through the metal and wiring of the corridor's ceiling, missing the creature entirely. "Time to move!" he ordered.

Shannon popped the airlock and dove through it with Vincente hot on his heels. The Aardvark was waiting for them, the engine idling fast. It had moved closer to the ship, but the armor was up and the doors were not open. Vincente began to yell into the comm.

"Melts! Get that damn door open! We're coming in hot! Melts? Melts! Come in, Melts!" The side door of the APC remained closed. Vincente swore. "Hector, we got a problem. I can't get Melts on the horn!"

"Shannon, handle it," the mercenary ordered over the comm. Shannon moved past Vincente and raised his carbine. He pounded on the door twice with the butt of the carbine, then once, then three times. The APC hatch popped open immediately, revealing an armed and terrified looking Melts. Shannon pushed the barrel of Melts' gun away from his face before he could accidentally shoot his comrades. Melts had the look of someone who had just walked through Hell itself.

"About time!" Vincente snarled as he and Shannon hurried on board. Hector came last, his rifle pointed back towards the ship. He ducked inside and Melts slammed the door shut as soon as Hector was aboard. As soon as the door was secure, Melts was already moving as fast as he could for the driver's seat.

"Something is out there," he called over his shoulder at them.

"No shit?" Vincente asked, sarcastically. He suddenly realized that the interior of the APC stank. He cupped a hand over his nose and snarled. "What the hell is that smell?"

"Feces and blood," Melts replied in a tight voice. "Something got Jacob and tore him in half."

Only then did Vincente notice the lower half of Jacob's body lying on the Aardvark's floor beneath the turret hatch. Bloated strands of intestines leaked from the rendered and torn flesh of what remained of the lower half of Jacob's torso. The dead mercenary's pants were stained dark with blood and something else. Vincente felt sick and his stomach threatened to empty what little it had onto the deck. He swallowed and managed to keep it down.

He grabbed hold of the support bar on the wall as the Aardvark lurched into motion. Melts had put the hammer down. Hector barely managed to brace himself as Vincente had. Shannon was flung violently to the floor. He landed with a wet noise on top of the mess that had been Jacob. A string of curses erupted from Shannon as the Aardvark's momentum balanced out and he sunk a hand into Jacob's blood-soaked bowels as he had tried to get back to his feet.

"Oh, sweet mercy," Shannon whispered. "I think I just squished his spleen."

****

Vincente paused to catch his breath after relating the story. "We drove straight here at the Aardvark's max speed. Several of those things chased us for a while, too."

Hector started to say something, but Vincente cut him off.

"You bloody well know they did. Just because we couldn't see them didn't mean they weren't there. I know you heard those things, just like I did. Like we all did."

"We did hear things," Hector confessed. He didn't go into any more detail than that.

"Tell me you at least brought back some of the parts we need," Jasmine asked.

Vincente shook his head. "No time, and there wasn't that much there anyway. That ship was in no way compatible with ours. Trust me on this."

He handed her the downloaded data from the ship. Jasmine glanced over it. "And this is for real?"

"Afraid so," Vincente told her. She nodded and plugged the datapad into the banks of their ship. She quickly read the data and frowned.

"According to this, a few of these monsters are three hundred feet tall," she blinked, as if some connection inside her head had just been made.

Vincente recognized the far-away look. "You got something?"

"Holy..." she trailed off. "We didn't crash."

Vincente wondered if she'd lost it for a moment. "Uh, yeah we did. I was there. Mostly."

"On our way down," Jasmine explained. "Something hit us and knocked us out of the air. We thought it was lightning, but what if it wasn't? Don't you see? That explains the damage to the Fancy's hull, and it explains just why that storm seemed to intensify the moment we started coming down."

Jasmine turned and called up a detailed holographic image of the damage to the Fancy above her own datapad. She pointed at the hull. "Look closely. The damage... it's like a giant set of claws cut into the hull."

"Frag, she's right," Shannon said.

"See?" Vincente almost laughed. "We're all dead, just like I told you. The only hope we have of getting the parts we need to get the Hell out of here are one hundred and fifty miles away. Do you think those things are just going to sit around and let us drive over there to pick them up? Even if the Fancy were fully operational, I wouldn't want to put her against one the bigger creatures in straight up combat, much less the Aardvark. One of the big ones could squash it like a bug."

"Shazu," Kamol whispered in an awed tone as he took the downloaded data from Jasmine and began to look over it himself.

"So we just sit here and wait from them to come and kill us?" Jasmine challenged Vincente and Hector. "I don't think so."

"Lady has a point," Yolo backed Jasmine up. "Sounds like we're dead whatever we do, so we might as well go out fighting."

Hector slapped Yolo on the shoulder. "To the last man."

Yolo smiled at his CO. "To the last man."

"Well, aren't we the proud men of Lord Cardigan," Vincente threw his up his hands. "It's a good day to die and all that junk. I hear you. What the Hell? It might even be fun. At the very least, maybe we can take some of those monsters with us."

"Into the valley of Death rode the Six Hundred," Melts murmured. "Fitting, actually."

"We're gonna need a plan," Shannon said.

Vincente manned up, getting it together. Besides, what else was there to do?

"Jasmine, you and Shannon go over that data on the monsters. If they have weaknesses that the Zebulun or the military know about, I want to know about them, too. Kamol, I want the Fancy's weapon system online with the shields, yesterday. If those things show up, let's not make it easy for them. Hector, you and Melts are with me."

"Doing what?" Melts asked.

"Making the biggest damn bomb we can," Vincente smiled. "Maybe we can't kill one of the big ones but with a bit of luck and creativity, maybe we can blow its freaking foot off if it tries to step on us."

"Don't you mean 'when?'"

CHAPTER EIGHT

"I think I finally figured out why the reactive skin isn't sealing the holes made by the creature when we crashed," Jasmine said as she poked her head into the cargo bay. Melts, Shannon and Vincente were working on a large cylindrical drum in the center of the room. They were surrounded by a mass of tangled wires and cuttings, and the two mercenaries were staring at Vincente. More precisely, their eyes were locked on the wire cutters in Vincente's hand.

"Not now," Vincente told her. "Going to see if I blow us all up now or later."

"Red wire is hot," Melts said in a low voice.

"I hope this works," Shannon added.

Vincente nodded and clipped off two blue wires. With Melts' assistance, he then joined the two wires with a yellow. Exhaling slowly, Shannon nodded and they released all of the wires. The smaller mercenary looked over the wiring and grunted in satisfaction. He turned and tested the power source, which read green. His lips were thin as he smiled.

"Everything looks green on this end," he reported. "Gentlemen... and lady, I think we've got a bomb."

"How much time would we have?" Jasmine asked, her own news forgotten as she stared at the drum. "And what are you using as a catalyst?"

"We'd have twenty-five minutes," Shannon told her. "If we aren't two miles out by then, we're dead. As for the catalyst, it's tritium that we drained from the reactors. I'm doing a single stage gun-barrel compression. We don't have the time for spherical."

"Wait, you built a nuke?" Jasmine asked, shocked.

"Well, yeah," Shannon shrugged.

"Where'd you get the enriched material? How'd you shape the implosion charge?"

"Kamol, the alien? He had about three pounds of enriched plutonium in engineering. I'm not asking why he had it, or from where he got it, but I think we are going to get along. We're not imploding, we're compressing! Gun barrel, remember? Little boy style. We used the RDX from the main gun shells as the compressor. From there, it was all just a matter of knowing how to build it," Shannon explained. "Which I know how."

"You think a nuke will harm it?"

"Not as much as a nuke exploding at one thousand feet would," Shannon admitted. "I'd rather this went off right in from of their faces, but I'm working with limited material here. We've looked at the wind direction and found that if we do have to blow up the Fancy, the fallout won't take it anywhere near the other ships. A ground explosion will be muted, hence the two mile buffer I want. But I'd kill to get an airburst out of this thing..."

"You built a nuke," Jasmine smiled. "I'm impressed."

"You have no idea how hard that is, impressing her," Vincente told the confused mercenary. He looked back at his pilot. "You said you had something?"

"Oh, right, look," she said and brought up the schematics of the ship once more on her datapad. "The holes aren't fixing themselves because there is some sort of enzyme on the hull interfering with the healing process. I'm willing to bet that when Genshi nailed us, he had some sort of reactive poison on his claws."

"Genshi?" Melts asked.

"Apparently, the other ship gave the Kaiju code names," Jasmine explained. "Genshi isn't the largest, but he's pretty damn big. He is sort of an elemental-like beast with plasma running along his spine and torso. They didn't have a good picture of him for some reason, but they had his size and what he does. We didn't run into a storm or something, we ran into him. And he hit us."

"Would that also block our comms?" Vincente asked.

"That's a good bet," Jasmine said. "There's some sort of static field around him, which screws up comms and sensors. That's a good thing, though."

"I can't see how this is a good thing," Vincente complained.

"Think about it, boss. Our comms go wacky, and we know that Genshi's near."

"Oh," Vincente nodded. "Good point."

"There were seven big ones total," Shannon reminded her. "What are the others like?"

"We have data on six only," Jasmine shrugged her shoulders. "Don't blame me. They just have one listed as Granddaddy, and he's the biggest. That's all. The others have names, their physical traits, and their territorial space."

"So did you figure out which one they were trying to force into their ship yet?" asked Vincente.

"There are two possibilities," Jasmine said. "Hacks and Kage. Both of them are the right size to fit into the cage, and their territories are practically touching where the ship is parked. Hacks weighs in at about four tons, and is a rock-solid multi-coloured thing with claws, teeth and feathers. Kage is dark, but much smaller, almost man-sized, maybe a little bigger. He's more into stealth than show, according to the notes. I don't have a lot of info on them, just size and potential usage on both. I'd say that the military set down precisely where they intended, and that they didn't crash like we'd been told."

"Surprise, surprise," Vincente's scowl was dark. "I was lied to. Shocked. I am shocked and appalled, I am."

"Those guys are bad, but they're not the immediate problem," Jasmine said as she flipped through the datapad. She brought up a fresh image and turned it into a hologram. "These guys are the problem."

Said creature was small, perhaps three feet in length and a mouth filled with long, pointed teeth. They had short, stubby forearms and skin, which looked like brightly-colored snake scales. Their claws were murderously sharp, and their eyes burned with a keen intelligence. They had no back legs. The creature looked soft to the touch, but looks, all of them knew, were oftentimes deceiving.

"They just called this guy Inky," Jasmine said. "It moves like a snake, but it is as fast as a man, maybe faster. It apparently resides in Hacks' territory, or perhaps it is the spawn of Hacks. Not sure. They're drones, though, like ants, but they are very protective of him, like protecting the queen. Probably the best analogy I can come up with. I'm willing to bet that's what got Jacob."

"You'd lose that bet," Melts muttered, his voice low. "Whatever got Jacob was faster than I could see, and had black scales. I think it could fly, too."

"There was something similar in the ship, too," Shannon added. "It was black, though."

"Well, there goes that theory," Jasmine sighed. "I'll keep digging and see what else they had. Maybe I can find more out about... whatever it was that hit the APC."

"You're doing fine," Vincente reassured her.

"You know how I get when I can't fix something," Jasmine said. She thought for a moment, then added, "or break anything."

"How's fuel for the Aardvark?" Vincente asked, changing the subject. Jasmine made a motion for him to follow, so he did. They ducked into the damaged cockpit and closed the door.

"We're good there, actually," she said. "I'd say about fifteen, twenty hours left at full power. Four to six days on half. I can always pilfer fuel from the Fancy as well, though that means we're not getting off this planet at all."

"The odds aren't good that we're getting off in one piece," Vincente groused. "I'm wondering if any of the other ships crashed as well, or if they're like the military vessel and fine." He stopped and stared at the ruined pilot controls, realization dawning on him. "Wait... that ship is parked there."

"Yeah," Jasmine nodded.

"That means it didn't crash," Vincente explained, excitement growing. "We can kill whatever that thing that was inside, right? Why not just steal that ship?"

"Two reasons," Jasmine said as she held up her fingers. "One, there's a strange black creature on board that probably killed everyone there. Who knows how many others are on board as well. Two, their navcomputers are trashed. Standard operating procedure is to dump the nav charts when the ship is deemed lost, especially when its one of these 'research vessels.' I'm surprised that they didn't slag everything, truth be told."

"They probably died before they could finish the job," Vincente said.

"Did you find any bodies?" Jasmine asked. Seeing him shake her head, she continued. "Probably just as well. I hate it when I find half-chewed up bodies."

"How are our navcomputers?"

"Fried," she said. "The plasma charges of Genshi overloaded our relays. I thought about that, too. Vincente... I hate to say it, but the Fancy's never leaving this place."

He sighed. "Mister Ambrose is going to have my head."

"You could always give him the ship we might steal," Jasmine said.

"You said that our navcomputers are fried," he reminded her. "How're we supposed to get out of here without them?"

"There are five or six other ships out there, Vincente," Jasmine said. "Maybe we'll get lucky?"

"You know how my luck usually runs," he said. "It's a word that is never associated with anything positive."

"But my luck..." her voice trailed off as she smiled.

****

"Look, captain, I want to get off this rock as badly as you, but what you're proposing... it's almost certainly suicide," Hector said as he rested his elbows on the edge of the table.

"Maybe," Vincente allowed as he looked at the gathered mercenaries and crew. Even Kamol, who normally abhorred group meetings, was watching, albeit from the doorway near engineering. "But sitting here, waiting for whatever else is out there, is definitely suicide."

Nobody could meet his gaze and deny the truth. The weather on Gorgon IV had grown steadily warmer throughout the day, which Jasmine had finally pegged at forty standard hours. Twenty of daylight, and twenty of darkness, she told them. The hotter it became outside, the warmer the interior of the Fancy became. Water, which they had plenty of, would be used much faster if they stayed inside the ship. The Aardvark, while not nearly as safe as the Fancy, was better powered and somewhat cooler.

The fact remained, though that they were going to die on the Gorgon IV unless they did something. The planet was more than living up to its moniker as Murder World, and although Vincente was loathe to admit it, he had made a huge mistake. Blundering into a dangerous situation was one thing, but allowing oneself to be blinded by greed and ignoring all of the dangers willfully was another matter in itself. He had brought this onto his crew and the mercenaries, and he was ultimately responsible for everything, which could or had already happened to them. For the time being, though...

None of them wanted to die, not on this forsaken planet. Vincente knew this, and used it to his advantage. He had to because he had no other choice. "You don't want to die, despite your pretty words about to the end. I know, because I've been delaying my meeting with St. Peter for the longest time. In order to do that, though, we need to think outside of the box. And while I'm all for blowing up the Fancy to hurt one of these creatures, I really don't want her death to be for nothing. She's been a good ship."

"Not to mention the amount of money that you've put into the electronics and weaponry out of your own pocket," Jasmine chimed in helpfully.

"And that," Vincente allowed. "I'd hate to see all that money be wasted on something small."

"But... that much distance, in the Aardvark alone, just to look at some ships which may have the part we need to steal a secret military ship–"

"Salvage, Hector," Vincente corrected the mercenary. "This has become a salvage operation."

"Fine," Hector nodded. "Salvage a secret military ship that was designed to kidnap a god worshipped by one of humanity's greatest enemies and get off a planet that, if you believe the legends, nobody ever has."

"Somebody has gotten off this planet," Jasmine interjected.

"How do you know that?" Yolo asked.

"Because the military knew enough to send in a ship that was already built for this sort of thing," she explained. "So obviously, they scouted this place extensively."

"So how can we be certain that these ships are worth salvaging?" Hector asked.

Vincente shook his head. "We don't, but we have to try."

"Okay," Hector finally agreed. "Let's grab our gear and get going. How long until that nuke goes off?"

"I haven't set it yet," Shannon answered, slightly embarrassed. "I wanted to make sure we were actually leaving."

"Okay, do it," Hector said. "Kamol, get the Aardvark up and ready. Grab only what you can carry on you, unless it's ammo. The APC can carry eight, not counting the driver and the turret gunner, so we'll use the extra space to store ammo. Make sure it's secure."

"Make sure you're kitted out in your battle armor," Vincente told them. "It'll provide extra protection if something goes wrong. Let's go, people. Time's a-waiting."

Everyone broke away at a brisk pace. Jasmine brushed past Yolo as she walked into her wardroom. She began stripping off her shirt, uncaring that she was giving the big mercenary a show. He leaned against the doorframe and crossed his arms. He smiled as she turned around.

"Why are you staring? They're just boobs," Jasmine asked.

"Which I lack, and therefore am interested in them. Specifically perky ones like yours."

"Shut up and hand me my battle armor."

"That's the sexiest thing I've ever heard."

"Battle armor. Now."

"Okay," he said as he raised his hands in surrender. He grabbed the thin vest that was resting on a metal hook just inside the hatch and tossed it to her. She caught it and slid it on, zipping up the front. She pulled her long hair up and activated the armor. The soft, flexible pads were now reactive to any forceful impact, which could hurt her. She tapped her ribs hard to check. The pads instantly became rigid before going soft again, the force of the blow absorbed and the energy diverted. She nodded and pulled on a fresh shirt.

"No pants armor?" Yolo asked, surprised. She looked at him and smiled sweetly.

"I always wear it."

"You," Yolo murmured as she walked past him, and out of the room, "are a classy dame."

"That's the sweetest thing you've said yet. There may be hope for you after all."

"So that means you like me," Yolo smiled.

"It means I won't kill you," she amended, "yet. You need to get your gear."

The mercenary nodded. "Thanks for the show."

"Jackass," she grumbled at the man's back.

Ten minutes later, she was back in the cockpit of the Fancy. Next to her, Shannon was doing one final check of their surroundings before they headed off in search of the other ships. She vented the fuel tanks around the Fancy that they couldn't take with them, hoping to give an extra kick to their explosion in case the nuke fizzled. Satisfied, she looked back over at Shannon.

"Anything?" she asked as Vincente leaned into the cockpit.

"Not sure," Shannon replied. "Some intermittent interference. Surges and pulses, you know? Uncontrolled."

"Sounds familiar," Jasmine nodded. "I think it's about time."

"I think you're right," Vincente said.

"I'm getting something," Shannon said. Jasmine began to look over the scanners with him. "I'll be damned if they're going all gobbledegook on me."

"The interference is getting stronger," Jasmine said. She turned and looked at Vincente. "Genshi is coming, and from the power surges I'm getting, he's coming in quick."

"Time to move, people," Vincente ordered. "Hector, get everyone down to the Aardvark."

"Who's triggering the bomb?" Shannon asked as he got up from his seat.

"I'll rig the timer," Vincente said. He reached out and patted the bulkhead lovingly. "Gotta say goodbye to the old girl."

"You know how?" Jasmine asked him as she pushed past. "Wait, never mind. Just don't take too long. We don't have a large window here, boss."

Vincente watched her leave before tracing his hand lovingly along the dashboard. He sighed deeply and looked around the cockpit, where he had spent a lot of his non-drinking time. He knew every nook and cranny on her, better than he had known any woman. It was strange to think of the ship as anything more than a common transport, but Vincente had spent too much time with the Fancy to think of her as anything less than what she truly was: a part of him.

"You were a good ship," he said. "The best, actually. Never seen one like you, and there'll never be another like you again. Got me out of a few scrapes, and no matter how much I asked of you, you never said no. I'm sorry... sorry that it has to end this way. You should be in space, flying amongst the stars, free. Thanks for taking care of me, old girl. I'll never forget you."

Vincente walked down to the cargo bay where the nuke was set. He knelt down, and with a deep breath, triggered the fifteen minute timer. The device immediately began to count down. He stood, brushed off his pants, and looked around. The mercenaries had picked the room clean, and not a stray round of ammunition could be found. Another sigh. It was hard to leave his ship. He moved across the cargo bay and into the adjoining bay, closing the hatch behind him. The others were already on board the Aardvark and the light from outside was spilling into the exposed bay.

The ground shook slightly. Vincente stopped and frowned, wondering if he had imagined it. Nothing happened for a moment, so he continued. The ground shook again.

"Hector? You feel that?" Vincente asked as he clambered inside the Aardvark. Hector looked behind them and stopped. His eyes grew wide as his mind struggled to take in the large shadow that loomed.

A second Kaiju had appeared in the distance on the open side the downed Fancy. It was monstrous in size, and was bigger and bulkier than Jasmine had said the Genshi would be. Vincente swallowed and looked at Hector, who shook his head.

"Of course, there'd be some sort of pissing contest between two big assed Kaiju right when we're about to leave," Vincente complained as he threw his hands upwards towards the sky. "Seriously, is it because I stopped going to church?"

CHAPTER NINE

As Genshi screamed a challenge at the new arrival, Hector secured the side door of the Aardvark. Satisfied that it was locked, he shifted his rifle across his knees and leaned forward.

"You got anything on this new one," he asked Shannon. The small mercenary looked at Jasmine for help.

"Razorface," she supplied as she flipped the image of the new Kaiju into a hologram. "Same size as Genshi, though he seems to be more solidly built. They called him that because he has four mouths and a tongue that... well now. If not for the barbed teeth on that thing, it could make a girl very happy."

A shrill, answering scream came in reply to Genshi's challenge. Every head in the Aardvark looked up instinctively, though they could not see what was going on. After sharing a sheepish look, they looked back at Jasmine, who continued.

"He's far from his normal range, which says that this is a territorial fight," she confirmed the captain's earlier suspicions. She chewed on her bottom lip for a moment as she read. "Huh. I wonder what happens when one kills the other?"

"Makes our escape easier?" Hector tried. "Who cares? Let's get out of here while we still can."

"Contact!" Melts called from the driver's seat. "I've got thousands of those little multi-colored buggers in front of us. I think those are the ones that belong to Genshi. I need someone up top on the turret!"

Yolo shook his head. "I don't fit."

"No way," Shannon said. "I saw what was left of Jacob. No thanks."

"You're such a little whiny..." Jasmine's muttering trailed off as she passed her smaller carbine off to Yolo. She put on the helmet and checked her shoulder holster to make sure her sidearm was still there. She tossed the datapad to Shannon. "There better not be a scratch on that thing when I come back in."

She slammed open the hatch and stuck her head outside. She immediately ducked down as something clanged loudly on the roof. She swore, whipped out her sidearm and popped back up.

Two loud gunshots punctuated her actions. She ducked her head back inside.

"Razorface's little buggers are pretty much big brown dogs with chainsaws for mouths," she explained. "They're cute and dangerous. I think I want one, if they'd stop trying to eat my face."

"You're insane, you know that, right?" Hector asked. Jasmine smiled blissfully.

"How sweet. You care. You really care."

"Turret," Vincente ordered, struggling to keep a straight face. "Now." In spite of all the dangers and their imminent death, Jasmine could still make him smile.

She stuck her tongue out at him and popped back into the turret. Moments later, the large guns began hammering out rounds into the approaching horde of the smaller beasts. An occasional shell casing dropped into the APC as Melts threw it into gear.

"Rolling out!" he cried. "Going at half speed so we can conserve fuel in case we run into something on the way."

"I've already plugged the coordinates in for you," Shannon told him. "Just follow them."

"I figured as much!" Melts yelled back as the APC began to accelerate. He pounded a fist on the roof of the cabin. "Hang on up there!"

Jasmine heard him, but did not have time to reply. She began to shoot the turret's guns in measured bursts as they drew closer to the fighting Inkys. The new arrivals, dark brown in color and matching Razorface's distinct features, began to rip into the horde of Inkys. She ducked down as an Inky leapt atop the moving APC, teeth covered in saliva and blood. It let loose a horrible scream.

"Damn it," she muttered and whipped out her pistol from the shoulder holster. She fired twice, knocking the Inky from view with one shot. She quickly swiveled the turret around and unloaded into a large cluster of Inkys and the other creatures, laying waste to both groups of beasts. Body parts and blood flew as the explosive rounds of the APC's turret connected with scaly, alien skin.

Something heavy slammed into her shoulder. The gun was knocked from her hand and it started to slide away on the roof. Her left hand shot out to grab it while her right grabbed the kukri she had strapped to her chest. As her fingers wrapped around the grip of the pistol, she slammed the kukri down, impaling the shoulder of another Inky. The creature howled in surprise and pain as the kukri slammed it down to the roof. She brought the pistol back and fired, point-blank, directly between the creature's eyes. She jerked the kukri out and the creature slid off the roof, dead.

Shoulder throbbing with pain from the impact of the Inky, she pivoted and drove her pistol straight into the mouth of another which had been about to rip her unprotected neck open. She saw the intelligence, fury and surprise in those bright eyes before she ended its life with a bullet.

As quickly as they had appeared, both species of small Kaiju were gone. Jasmine felt the Aardvark lurch slightly as it shifted gears. Melts must have recognized the sudden emptiness in front of them and increased speed slightly. Nothing else attacked them as they motored parallel and slightly away from the carnage-filled battlefield. Jasmine looked back at the Fancy, her own mental timer counting down as they drove away.

Her eyes widened as she watched Razorface come within range of Genshi. Electricity crackled up and across the breastplate of the armored Kaiju as Genshi let rip into Razorface's heavier body. Undaunted, each mouth of Razorface opened and grabbed onto the exposed shoulder of the other Kaiju. Genshi let loose a scream of pain and anger as Razorface ripped a massive chunk of carapace and flesh out. Blood gushed from the wound, but instead of weakening it, the injury only seemed to infuriate Genshi. A larger bolt of lightning exploded out from the mouth of the Kaiju and drove through the chest of Razorface.

Razorface faltered and staggered back. He whipped his tail around, and Jasmine saw that the tip was not a slender point like normal tails, but more like a heavy club with massive spikes. The tail swung wide, but Genshi was ready for it. He lifted one massive foot and blocked the thicker half of the tail. He then ripped downward with his claws, creating a long gash in Razorface's tail. The heavier Kaiju howled in fury and slammed a shoulder into the midsection of his opponent. Genshi staggered backwards and the wounded Razorface pressed the advantage, bringing his wounded tail into play again.

The club swung high and clipped Genshi across the back of his reptilian-like head. More blood flew as a spike managed to gouge the thick plating in the back of his head. Razorface stuck his maw into the abdomen of Genshi and began to use his tongue and mouths to rip open the other Kaiju. Genshi howled in fury and pain, and the lightning around the two began to intensify. A claw lashed out and slammed into the side of Razorface's head, drawing more blood. Razorface stepped back and Genshi hit him with another bolt of lightning. Both combatants roared and took a small step back to reassess their opponent.

Jasmine's mental countdown reached zero. She quickly dove inside the APC and slammed the turret shut.

"Melts, close your eyes now!" she screamed.

"What?" Melts called back as a new sun suddenly exploded on the horizon.

The APC swerved wildly as Melts jerked the wheel. The Aardvark, not designed for sharp maneuvers, tilted. Everyone inside tumbled to the left as the wheels on the right side came up off the ground. Melts, blinded and in pain, continued to pull on the wheel, causing the vehicle to list further.

"Yolo!" Jasmine shouted and tried to shove the big mercenary towards the opposite side. He understood immediately but did not have enough time to react. The APC's rugged wheels finally caught in the sand and the momentum of the heavy Aardvark tipped it over.

The side of the APC slammed into the ground, causing everyone inside to crash into the side door. Another tumble scattered everything inside as the Aardvark was – briefly – upside down before it was upright again. It tipped again, but did not flip over a second time. The engine coughed for a moment, then died. Too much fuel in the pistons prevented them from firing.

The shockwave from the nuclear explosion caught up to them, the heavy wind buffeting the APC and cracking the windshield. The vehicle rocked back and forth again, and for a moment, it looked as though they would end up permanently on their side. The fury of the windstorm abated after a few seconds, leaving the immediate area filled with a terrifying stillness.

One of the side doors of the Aardvark had swung open. Cautiously, Vincente climbed over the unconscious form of Yolo and pushed the door open a little wider. He poked his head out and saw the massive mushroom-shaped cloud climbing into the sky in the distance. He sighed and wiped a sudden tear from his eye. Of the Kaiju, there was no sign.

"Two miles, eh?" Vincente asked. Shannon groaned painfully.

"I may have underestimated the yield a bit," the mercenary admitted after struggling to take a deep breath. "I think I may have broken a rib, too."

Vincente came back in and reset the door. He moved over to Hector, who waved him off. The mercenary leader was mostly uninjured, though he was cradling his left wrist to this chest. Kamol was next to him, the alien grumbling under his breath in heavily accented Lorn about the horrible driving of humans. Yolo had a nasty gash on his head but seemed otherwise okay, and Jasmine had as usual, escaped the carnage practically unscathed. Vincente climbed forward to check on their driver.

Melts was an absolute wreck. He had not fastened his safety harness before the Aardvark flipped, and had been tossed around in the cabin. The jagged white edge of bone had broken through the skin in his shoulder, and while the shirt he was wearing compressed it enough to staunch the flow of blood, it was doing nothing more to protect the injury. His face was covered in small cuts and more blood matted his hair.

The worst damage, though, was to his eyes. The pupils had been completely burned out from the intense light emitted by the explosion. It wouldn't normally have been that bad, but the mercenary had happened to be staring directly at the ongoing battle between the Kaiju. In spite of Jasmine's warning, Melts had not managed to look away in time. Blindness was certain, and even with modern technology, Vincente wasn't sure that they'd be able to reconstruct the pupils to what they were before.

"Jasmine!" Vincente called out. "Med kit!"

"Oh jeez," she hissed as she pushed her way forward and looked at Melts' ruined face. She whipped out a tranquilizer and injected it into his thigh. Gingerly, she hooked her arms beneath his and began to pull the injured man out of the chair. The broken shoulder rose and fell, and she winced as the edge snagged on the seat. Melts didn't make a sound though, for which she was extremely grateful. She looked back over her shoulder. "Hector, grab your man!"

The mercenary leader took the heavier weight from Jasmine and carefully slid him onto the floor of the Aardvark. Vincente pushed past Jasmine and climbed into the front seat. He tried the engine. It turned but refused to start. He pushed down on the accelerator and pumped it a few times before turning the ignition again. Still nothing.

"What the hell is wrong with this thing!?" he roared, frustrated. He pounded on the steering wheel and tried it again.

"You're flooding it, you twit!" Jasmine snapped back. "Let the engine rest for five minutes and try it again."

"We don't have the time!"

"Then make it!" Jasmine answered. "Kamol, get up here and drive. Don't let him flood the engine any more than it already is. Somebody wake Yolo up. Two of you cover the gun ports. I'm taking the turret again. Any questions?"

"None from me, ma'am," Hector grinned. "Shannon? Wake up our boy."

The small mercenary reached into the med kit and pulled out a small tab. He broke it and shoved it under the big man's nose. Two seconds passed before Yolo rolled onto his side and dry heaved. He pushed himself up off the floor and looked around.

"We lived," came the observation. "Cool."

"Hold on there, big guy," Shannon said. He held up his fingers. "How many am I holding up?"

"Before or after I break them and feed them to you?"

"He's fine," Shannon smiled. He handed Yolo the heavy machine gun. "Driver's side gun port. Shoot anything that looks dangerous."

"Didn't we just nuke the place?"

"Maybe it turned the Kaiju into super Kaiju," Hector said. "Doesn't matter. Get on the gun port."

"All right, sorry," Yolo muttered and slid forward. Jasmine waited for him to move before she climbed into the turret. She checked her comms and found to her surprise that the interference that was there before was now gone. She smiled and activated the comms.

"The EMP from the nuke didn't burn out the comms," she stated. "Vincente, you still in the driver's seat? Get out of there and tell everyone to get their helmets back on. We've got comms. See if the sensors are up and running again."

"They are," he replied instantly. "Good work."

"I didn't do anything," she said. "I just figured that since Genshi is gone the interference must be—"

"Contact!" Yolo shouted and opened fire, letting loose a continuous stream of fire behind her. Jasmine turned the turret around and felt her stomach drop. A large, brown wave of the smaller Kaiju were rushing towards the APC. Apparently, these were the reserves for Razorface.

"It's never easy, is it?" Vincente asked as he moved to the back of the Aardvark. Moving cautiously around Melts, he grabbed a duffel bag fill with extra ammunition. He brought the magazines over to Yolo and sat next to him. "Get your helmet on! Got some ammo for you!"

"Thanks!" Yolo said loudly as he continued to fire. "Seventy round mags. God bless illegal arms dealers!"

"Don't let the Wild Ones hear you call them that," Vincente said as he passed a fresh magazine to Yolo. He grabbed the large helmet hanging near Yolo's head and slapped it on the big mercenary. "They take that sort of thing personally."

"Helmet, right," Yolo grunted. "Now I don't have to yell."

"Lots of them?" Vincente asked as he tried peeking over Yolo's shoulder to see outside.

"Yeah."

"Crap." Vincente leaned towards the front of the Aardvark. "Kamol, get this thing going!"

"Kershea lungo dou?"

"I have no idea, just do it!"

"Shazu."

The engine began to reluctantly turn over, but the spark wouldn't catch. Vincente heard the distinct war cry of a Lorn, followed by what he could only guess was something heavy hitting the control panel of the APC, then the ignition turn over again.

This time, the engine rumbled to life, albeit for a moment. It coughed, backfired, and died.

Overhead, the gun turret joined in with Yolo's incessant firing, creating a massive wall of rounds, which punched into the oncoming horde. Dozens upon dozens of the mini Razorface's died each second, but still they came. One hundred yards. Eighty. Sixty.

"Kamol!" Vincente shouted as they got within forty yards. "Anytime now would be great!"

The big engine coughed again and fired up, rumbling loudly and, more importantly, steadily. The Lorn gunned the engine and slammed it into gear as the first wave of the Kaiju reached the armored vehicle.

The mouths of the miniature Razorfaces attached themselves to the metal of the Aardvark and methodically began to saw through the thick armor. A few bounced off as the vehicle picked up more speed, but at least ten were stuck to the armor that Vincente saw. He turned and looked over at Hector, who had been backing up Shannon at the other gun port.

"Flamethrower!" Vincente called out. "Do you have a flamethrower?"

"Yes, but I don't know where it is!" the mercenary responded quickly. "We have grenades, though."

"Jasmine!"

"Kinda busy, boss," came the terse reply.

"Not asking you to do anything but answer a question."

"Oh, I can do that."

Can grenades punch through our armor?" he asked.

"Probably not," she said. "The Aardvark was designed to withstand up to a HEAT anti-tank round."

"So a belt of grenades..." his voice trailed off questioningly.

"Should be– ow! Die, you little shit! " Blam! Blam! "–should be fine," she said. "Probably."

"Gimme a belt," Vincente said to Hector. The mercenary captain smiled and reached into his duffel bag.

"I got three. Was saving them for something special."

"I only need one."

Vincente accepted the grenades and looked them over. He shot a glance back at Hector. "Five second fuse?"

"Yep."

"Perfect." Vincente pushed Yolo aside and yanked out the pins. He counted to three and dropped the belt outside. He slammed the gun port shut. "Fire in the hole!"

Muffled explosions shook the APC. The gnawing sounds stopped. Yolo opened up the gun port and looked outside. The smoking remains of a few Kaiju were all that were left. There was a trail of dismembered bodies in their wake. Vincente smiled.

"That... was beautiful."

INTERLUDE IV

"Please state your name for the record."

"Kahuna Numero Uno Ragara, the Big Kahuna of Coyote Station," the Wild One seated across from the Prosecutor said in a low voice. He lifted a proud chin and stared defiantly at the smaller man across the table. Behind him, the guards tightened their grips on their weapons. "I am the leader of the Wild Ones, and you stole my space station."

"Merely occupied it with peacekeeping forces until this entire mess is smoothed over," the Prosecutor explained. "It's for your own protection. Vincente Huerta is a madman and a loose cannon. If he's still alive, he's a danger to you and your people. Besides, I'd like to ask you a few questions, that's all."

"I may not answer them."

"If you fail to comply, I can hold you in contempt and jail you."

"You already have my contempt, pissy man. Jail will be a nice vacation."

"I see," the Prosecutor smoothed his suit and looked at the torn and shoddy clothing, which adorned the proud leader. "I can get you better clothes. Clothes that don't... smell so much?"

"They say clothes make the man," Ragara said with a disrespectful snort. "I am a man who does not care what he wears, for he leads with strength. You are an insignificant man who wears expensive clothing to hide the fear, which drips from your body like blood from a spoiled virgin. You are afraid and you try to cover it. Poorly."

"You need to watch your tone!" the Prosecutor snapped. "I'll have these men beat you if you continue this!"

"Tell them to remember the safe word," Ragara challenged. "I don't want anyone to get hurt. Well, maybe you. A little."

"This isn't a game!" the Prosecutor said as he slammed his open palms down on the table. "People died, and we want answers!"

"People die every day," Ragara retorted. "Since when do men who hide in offices and wear fancy suits to hide their fears care about people other than themselves dying?"

"Since when do savages care in any case?"

"Call me what you will, but I will answer one question of yours."

"Only one, eh?" the Prosecutor leaned forward, eager. "Okay, I can agree to that. I'll let you go back to your little cell if you answer one question. And you swear to answer it?"

"Yes." Ragara crossed his arms, a strange smile on his face.

"Where is Vincente Huerta?"

"I already answered your one question," Ragara stated. The Prosecutor's face paled.

"What?"

"I already answered a question of yours. Our deal is done."

"I haven't asked anything!"

"Yes, you have," Ragara smiled, the gap between the remains of his two front teeth evident. "You asked if I would swear to answer it. I did."

"That doesn't count! That's not what I wanted to ask!"

"But it is what you asked," Ragara shrugged. "Foolish is the civilized man who underestimates the cunning of the barbaric one."

CHAPTER TEN

The Aardvark's engine roared as the APC streaked over the sand. Kamol was running it at fifty percent power, but even so, its speed was impressive. Vincente sat in the seat next to him, lost in thought. They'd been through so much already and still had hell itself to face before they had any hope of escaping Gorgon IV. He wasn't sure just how much more they could take before someone broke.

Melts was in bad shape. Jasmine told him that the odds of the scholarly mercenary ever seeing again were slim to none. The flash of the nuke had simply done too much damage to his unshielded eyes. The mercenary lay stretched out in the Aardvark's rear, and now that the immediate danger was gone, Jasmine was tending to him as best she could. Hector sat across from them, his head in his hands. The mercenary leader looked as exhausted as Vincente felt. Vincente could almost swear he saw new patches of grey in the man's hair. Hector's helmet rested on the seat beside him. Yolo sat near Hector, watching Jasmine. Shannon kept to himself, sitting at the extreme far end of the Aardvark, past the others, with his back to its rear wall. The little man appeared to be hard at work on the datapad in his hands. Vincente knew it was tied into the Aardvark's sensor array and also contained a copy of the data they'd downloaded on the Kaiju.

Shannon suddenly turned his head and looked towards the driver's compartment. "Incoming!" he screamed.

"Fuck me," Kamol muttered in perfect, unaccented English.

Something slammed into the side of the Aardvark, hitting it like a missile. The vehicle titled sideways, its right wheels, once again, leaving the sand. Its armored hull was dented inward from whatever struck it. Shannon was thrown from the floor, tumbling through the air to crash face first into the left side wall as Yolo attempted to catch the little man and failed. Jasmine was luckier. She had been crouching, close to the floor already, beside where Melts lay. She rolled with the impact to keep from being tossed about as the Aardvark's right wheels came back down onto the sand, jarring the whole vehicle. Melts tumbled towards her.

103

Vincente heard Jasmine grunt as his weight landed on her but he could see she wasn't really injured, merely irritated.

Hector and Yolo were on their feet, rifles in hand. Hector was heading for the turret as Yolo scrambled for the closest gun port. Vincente still couldn't see anything through the forward window. Kamol had kicked up the Aardvark's power to its max output and had his foot down on the accelerator.

"You speak English?" Vincente asked the alien. In all their years together, Kamol had never given any indication that he spoke Standard English as well as he understood it. Vincente shook off his shock and snapped out of his thoughts as his eyes jerked towards the windshield.

"What the hell was that?" Jasmine demanded, prying herself loose from underneath Melts' unconscious body. She checked his shoulder but spotted no additional damage from his surprise upending.

"Don't know!" Vincente shouted. "But according to the sensors, there's a lot more of them."

Jasmine rushed forward to stare at the screens over his shoulder. "Oh my..." she her voice faded.

Vincente finished for her. "They're in the air. Whatever they are, they're flying."

"Soneddia so paph," Kamol told them.

"What do you mean, a big shadow?" Vincente asked before he glanced up from the sensor data through the windshield again. Kamol was right though. The daylight outside was definitely dimmer. Where once there had been the bright rays of the planet's suns, now there was nothing but a shadowy cloak covering everything. It reminded Vincente of a solar eclipse. "That... is one big damned bird. Lion. Thing."

"Kaiju!" Jasmine shouted. "Shoot it!"

"Why is it here? How'd it find us?" Shannon demanded as he watched Hector clamber up into the turret.

"Does it really need a reason? Probably noticed the nuke we hit those other two with," Vincente grumbled. Outside, a piercing shriek echoed throughout, a familiar cry. His face paled. "So this thing was hunting us too? Damn. I need a drink."

"I got nothing on this one," Jasmine announced.

"What about the hundreds of the little bastards flying in the air around it?" Hector asked from above as the turret began to rotate. "Shit!"

Something large and leathery collided with the window. The thick, bulletproof windshield exploded inward. It clinked against the metal of the floor like rain as it came pouring down. Vincente managed to bring his arm up in time to protect his face. He could feel shards of the glass imbedding in his flesh. Jasmine was gone from sight. His best guess was that she'd used him and his seat for cover, ducking behind them.

The Kaiju was shaped like a large cat, though it had large, transparent wings. It stuck an oddly shaped head through the broken windshield and tried to attack Kamol. The Lorn reached beside where he sat bringing up a heavy wrench that met the Kaiju's elongated jaw with the sharp crack of bone as he swung it at the monster. The blow shattered the Kaiju's jaw, but did little to slow it down. Claws, several inches long, extended from the thing's hands. They tore into Kamol with a hellish zeal. Orange blood splashed over Vincente as the Kaiju ripped Kamol's chest apart.

Vincente jerked his pistol from the holster on his hip and leaned towards the Kaiju. He fired into the side of its head from point-blank range, time and time again, as the thing continued rend and shred Kamol's twitching body. If his shots did anything, it was only to piss the monster off more. It whirled on Vincente, a look of profound annoyance in its surprisingly intelligent eyes.

He was dead. There was nothing that could save him, and the Kaiju seemed to know this. It hissed, a low, guttural sound, which grew from the belly of the beast. Vincente swallowed and prepared for the worst. I really didn't want to go out like this, he thought as the second seemed to drag into an eternity. I wanted to go out on a beach somewhere while being fed grapes by a busty blonde or three.

The barrel of a rifle appeared in Vincente's peripheral vision. The barrel flashed as Yolo pulled the weapon's trigger and the Kaiju was flung back out of the Aardvark through the shattered window. Vincente slapped his hands over his ears as the sharp retort blasted his already-damaged eardrums, the massive sniper rifle deafening everyone inside. He felt the blast from the rifle in his heart, and it was an odd mixture or terrifying and ecstasy in the blast. As the large Kaiju toppled from view, Vincente saw the massive hole the shot had blown through its' central torso.

"Die you bastards!" Vincente faintly heard Hector's voice yelling over the comm. The turret atop the Aardvark had opened fire and was rotating back and forth above them.

Only then did Vincente realize that the Aardvark was still moving as the APC floundered about, zigging and zagging, across the sands of Gorgon IV. He started to make a move for the driver's seat but Jasmine was already in motion, having appeared out of nowhere once the Kaiju had disappeared. She yanked Kamol's body from it, which bounced onto the floor with a dull thud. She grimaced as she slid into the blood-soaked seat.

"I've got this!" she yelled at him. "Help the others in back!"

Vincente could still hear the turret firing above them and Yolo had rushed back to the gun port, his rifle spewing death through it. Vincente didn't have a rifle, and his pistol had proved useless against this new threat. Besides, I'd just be in their way, he told himself as he sprang from his seat and rushed to where Shannon and Melts lay in the rear of the Aardvark. Vincente could see that the little man was still breathing even before he rolled him over. Alive was good, but that was all that he could say about Shannon. His face was a bloodied mess. The force of being slammed into the Aardvark's wall had reduced his nose to... well, it wasn't a nose anymore, but rather a flattened mess of pulpy cartilage and skin. A bruise spread across Shannon's face reaching almost to the ears on either side. His upper lip was split open and there was blood everywhere. He saw that several of Shannon's teeth were gone as the little man tried to speak.

"Lummush," he spat through broken teeth and lips. "Lummush!"

"Shut up!" Vincente snapped. "Don't try to talk. Just hold on, okay?"

Vincente scanned the floor around him for the med kit but there was no sign of it. Only God knew where it had been flung to when the big Kaiju struck the Aardvark. Vincente knew there were other med kits in the emergency storage holds that were a part of the APC's walls. He left Shannon where he lay, darting for the closest one. Another, much smaller Kaiju collided with the APC, but this time Vincente was ready for it. He caught himself with his hands as the impact tossed him into the wall he'd been heading for. He fought with the latch on the hold, his fingers not wanting to work correctly from the fear coursing through him. For what seemed like forever, he struggled with the latch, swearing under his breath the entire time. Finally, it gave. He grabbed the med kit from the hold and threw himself back in Shannon's direction. Vincente heard someone screaming as he knelt down to attend to Shannon's wounds. One of the small Kaiju outside the APC had grasped the big man's forearm and was trying to pull him out through the small opening of the gun port. There was no sign of Yolo's rifle as the mercenary struggled in a tug of war with the Kaiju. Yolo's scream rose in pitch as he tore free of the thing's claws and flew backwards, leaving a trail of blood on the floor behind him that poured from the long, jagged grooves in the flesh of his forearm.

Steady bursts from the turret above told them that Hector was making short work of the smaller Kaiju still flying around. Leaderless now, they appeared to be less coordinated than before, though no less dangerous. Bodies continued to fall from the sky as the APC motored on towards their first destination.

As suddenly as it all began, it ended. Everything became still and quiet except for the sound of the Aardvark's engine and Yolo's pained curses.

"Lummush," Vincente called out to Jasmine once the shock of the sudden stillness wore off. "Shannon kept saying this. Does it make sense to you?"

"Lummox? Yes," Jasmine replied back loudly. "Yes it does. It was one of the seven."

"Well, damn," Vincente said. "I'd have traded that Kaiju if it meant that Kamol was still alive."

"Same here," Jasmine muttered under her breath. "Yolo? Quit being a bitch. You okay?"

Yolo grunted. "I'll live," he answered, clutching his mangled arm and holding it pressed to the armor covering his chest.

Jasmine asked "Hector, you still up there?"

The turret had gone silent like pretty much everything else outside. Hector didn't answer.

"Vincente! Go check on him!" Jasmine ordered.

"Why me?" Vincente argued before he could stop himself.

"Stop being a baby and get your shit together, man," Yolo said and nodded at something across the rear compartment from where Vincente knelt over Shannon. "Shannon's rifle is over there."

"Thanks," Vincente said sarcastically before going after it.

Like a man on death row being led from his cell, Vincente walked up to the turret hatch. Hector had closed and secured it behind him on his way up. That fact reminded Vincente of just what a professional Hector was. He pushed down on the small lever, which controlled entry into the turret and jumped back as it popped open. He took a deep breath and moved forward, thrusting his rifle upwards into the hatch against any threat that might be awaiting him there. The barrel of the rifle rammed into something soft and pliable.

"Ow! Chingada puta de madre!" Hector roared. "That was my balls!"

"Sorry!" Vincente apologized.

Hector slid from the turret onto the floor in front of Vincente, a long streak of blood trailing behind him on the turret ring. The mercenary's right arm was gone, and most of that shoulder was shredded beyond all recognition. Slashes cut from one of the smaller flying Kaiju's claws stretched over his face. His left eye dangled loosely from what remained of the socket. How in the hell Hector was even conscious with the extent of his wounds was a mystery to Vincente. The pain the mercenary must be in was unimaginable to him.

"Stop gaping at me and get a damned med kit!" Hector spat a large glob on blood onto the Aardvark's floor. "This combat stim isn't going to last forever."

"How'd you feel my... never mind," Vincente changed his mind as he helped the mercenary lean up against the wall of the APC. He tossed the rifle aside as he hurried to one of the compartments bolted to the interior wall of the Aardvark. He quickly fished out a wrapping and proceeded to wrap it around the end of the stump that used to be Hector's arm. He cut it and the wrapping hardened and constricted, effectively creating both a tourniquet and a bandage to protect the horrific injury.

Next, he gingerly prodded Hector's damaged eye back into the socket. It rolled in his fingers for a second before he managed to get it back in. He pressed his hand over the other eye so that the mercenary wouldn't be tempted to try to look in any direction and risk damaging the other eye any further. He slipped a patch over Hector's head and covered the good eye. Next, he bandaged the damaged one, and finally wrapped a clean cloth over both to keep the patch and bandage in place. He looked at Hector, who had nearly passed out at this point.

"I'm going to give you some pain meds now, Hector," Vincente told the mercenary leader. "You just relax. I've got you."

Vincente pulled the plastic cap off the needle and felt around in the crook of Hector's remaining elbow for a vein. Finding a good one, he smacked it twice before sliding the needle in. He felt the vein give way as the needle entered. Slowly, carefully, he began to inject the pain medicine.

Hector's head lolled to the side as the mercenary passed out from a combination of narcotics and blood loss. Vincente stood and hurried back up to the driver's compartment.

"Hector's secured, and doped up with the good stuff," Vincente said as he poked his head over Jasmine's shoulder. "ETA?"

"Two minutes, give or take," she said. "Skies are clear now that Yolo killed the big one, thankfully. I don't think we could handle another aerial assault. So... who's going to look in the big old ship?"

"You, me, Shannon," he replied. "Yolo is babysitting Hector and Melts."

"Sounds like a plan," Jasmine said. "What do we do... with Kamol?"

"Well," Vincente exhaled. "Lorn typically do... things to their dead. I'm not interested in doing that. So we'll get him back to the research ship and space him once we get out of here. His body will burn up on re-entry into the atmo, assuming we escape, I mean. Best I can do is not leaving him on this hellhole, you know?"

"Good idea."

"I'm just glad..." his voice trailed off as something large and bulky appeared to their right. He pointed as he recognized the blocky design of a cargo ship. "There."

"Got it," she said and turned the wheel. The APC slid slightly, and deftly maneuvering around a pile of rocks, she approached the ship from the nose. Vincente scouted for signs of Kaiju, but this area appeared abandoned.

"Well, we survived the first part," he exhaled.

"And to think," Jasmine said as they came to a stop next to the downed freighter, "that was supposed to be the easy part."

CHAPTER ELEVEN

The wind swept across the sandy surface of Gorgon IV, the sign of a massive dust storm brewing somewhere nearby. The tiny particles of sand made the view nearly impossible, especially with the windshield of the Aardvark completely destroyed thanks to Lummox. A fine layer of dust was beginning to form on the console and driver's seat. This, in turn, had forced Jasmine to grab protective goggles from one of the compartments for her eyes so that she could see where she was going.

Thankful that she had stashed a pair in the compartment, she used them to scan their surroundings. A few small shrubs dotted around the downed freighter, and a long, black gouge trailed behind. The freighter had obviously come down without power and crashed. She looked back at the cargo ship and whistled softly.

The "spine" of the ship was cracked, experienced eyes noticed immediately. The thrusters were also wrecked, and one of the stabilizer wings had snapped off somewhere during the ship's final descent. Scorch marks ran down the sides of the craft as well, and she spotted the telltale signs of laser burns at strategic spots on the ship. It had not crashed, she decided. It had been brought down.

"The information we stole did suggest that the Zebulun worshipped these Kaiju," Jasmine muttered. "Only makes sense that they'd offer a sacrifice or something."

"No worse than some old Earth civilizations," Vincente reminded her. "Everyone is barbaric in their own way. Think of the Wild Ones."

"Hey now," Jasmine countered in a soft tone. "They look at sex and violence in the same light. They will beat the crap out of one another, but they wouldn't feed their enemies to some monster on a planet."

That's because they don't have any monsters, he didn't say. Instead, he asked "You sure about that?"

"Yeah, I am."

"I'm glad you're confident in them," Vincente said with a sigh. "C'mon, let's get ready."

"I don't recognize that type of freighter," Jasmine admitted as she left the engine idling and exited the driver's seat. "You?"

"Not really," Vincente admitted. "Looks old."

"Might be because of the environment here," she told him. "The constant sand could weather it, make it look older."

"Thought about that," Vincente admitted, "but the choppy design, and the rounded stern of the ship where the rockets used to be? Yeah, not precisely modern."

"Didn't notice that," she said. "Hope they had decent nav computers."

"I hope they have any kind of navigation data," Vincente groused. "If they did a data dump as well, the next ship is damn near two hours south. I really don't want to go that far."

"Well, there's a freighter further to the west of here," she reminded him. "Ninety minutes away, but according to the maps in the other ship, there's a massive geological formation that hasn't been fully mapped yet due to seismic activity."

"Seismic activity?"

"Volcanoes."

"Oh, this place just gets better and better," Vincente growled.

"Nobody to blame but yourself, boss," Jasmine shrugged. "You ready to do this or what?"

"I guess," Vincente said as he moved towards the rear of the APC. There Shannon was waiting for them, most of the blood from his broken nose wiped away. Two small bruises had begun to form beneath his eyes, and his lips were still extremely swollen. However, he was alert and ready to go, which was something, Vincente decided.

"I can go with you," Yolo said as Vincente grabbed his rifle.

"Can't," he said. "Someone needs to watch the Aardvark and the guys. You're injured, but still functioning. Shannon is only mildly wounded. You get to stay."

"But I'm good!" Yolo protested.

"Can you carry your rifle and other things as well if it hits the fan in there?" Vincente asked. Yolo started to argue but Vincente cut him off. "No, you can't. I need two arms in there. You're still raring to go, I know, and I'm sorry. I need you out here."

"Damn it," Yolo whined.

"Relax, big guy," Jasmine said as she pat his good arm. "I'd rather not need you in there. If we did, then we're probably not walking out of that thing alive."

"Besides, if you want, you can wear the flamethrower," Vincente told him. Yolo's eyes lit up at that.

"We have a flamethrower? I thought you said you didn't know where it was!"

"Well, yeah," Jasmine nodded. "Too bulky for us to wear, but you look big enough to wear it."

"If you find it, and can get it on, it's yours," Vincente added.

"Cool!"

"You guys sure know how to handle him," Shannon said through broken lips as they disembarked from the APC. "Hector always had his hands full trying to manage the big guy. He's unbalanced, you know?"

"I gathered," Jasmine said. "It's why I pulled the gun on him, instead of hurting him more. I didn't expect him to go all baby duckling on me, though."

"Are we going to do this or what?" Vincente asked, exasperation in his tone. "We have six hours until the sun sets, and this dust storm is going to make returning to the spy ship that much more difficult."

"Okay, you ready?" Jasmine asked. Shannon nodded. "Good. No idea what sort of security locks there are, but..."

"I can handle whatever that old rust bucket can offer," the little mercenary reassured her.

"There's an airlock," Vincente said as they drew closer to the ruined freighter. He pointed. "Four feet up, forward of where the stabilizer wings used to be."

"Wow," Shannon said. "That's weird."

"What's weird?" Jasmine asked.

"I've never seen an airlock shaped like that before," Shannon explained. A moment later, he amended himself. "Well, outside of a text manual, that is."

"That old, huh?" Vincente shook his head. "Hope the air isn't contaminated."

"Spine's broke, boss," Jasmine said. "No way is that thing still airtight."

"All right," Vincente nodded. "Get us in, Shannon."

"Piece of cake," the mercenary grinned.

****

As it turned out, it was anything but.

"This should be a binary set solution," Shannon complained for the umpteenth time as he tried to hack into the console again. "This system is ancient. Why does it have an evolving algorithm as a pass code?"

Vincente coughed and pulled the cloth back up over his mouth so that he could breathe. The wind had grown stronger, which cut down on their ability to see. The tiny granules of sand assaulted them relentlessly, filling their hair, clothing, and ears. It threatened to fill their lungs, and would have if Vincente had not planned ahead.

"Breathing masks," he had said at the time. Simple cloth devices, which would cover the mouth and still allow air to get in, they were ingenious inventions, which still made communication between them easy. The other two had accepted them, albeit reluctantly.

Now, they were extremely thankful. Jasmine, eyes hidden behind her goggles, was staring out into the distance, trying to keep a lookout in case some other Kaiju were to show up. The scanners, which were working now that Genshi had been taken out of the picture, showed nothing other than the ship within ten miles. Beyond that, there was intermittent contact with smaller beings, but none were approaching them.

Still, the mask was mildly uncomfortable, designed for someone with a smaller face than the captain. Vincente wished that the mercenary would hurry up and crack the lock. The longer they were outside and exposed, the more dangerous it became. He was now intimately familiar with how dangerous Murder World truly was, and he figured his odds of surviving to get inside the freighter, at this rate, was less than forty percent. Plus, his mask was driving him nuts.

"Got it!" Shannon called out, triumphant. Vincente looked over, pleased. The airlock hissed and the small mercenary swung it open.

"I'll go first," Jasmine said. "Then Shannon, then Vincente. Comms are up with the Aardvark. Yolo, you still with us?"

"Check," the big man inside the APC responded. "Read you five by five."

"Why am I covering the rear?" Vincente asked, surprised.

"Because Yolo can see if something is coming, and there's only one way that we know to get on this ship," Jasmine said with a matter-of-fact tone. "If you're in the rear, you're in the safest spot."

"Right," Vincente nodded. Jasmine flipped on the light mounted on her rifle and slowly moved inside the freighter. Shannon followed and Vincente came in right behind him. He stopped and looked back out into the desert. "You want me to close this?"

"Go ahead," Shannon said. "It's easily opened from this side."

"Why isn't there any power to the ship," he wondered as he followed the others deeper into the bowels of the ship, "but the airlock still had power?"

"Two separate power sources, I suppose," Shannon offered. "In case there's a total ship catastrophe and power is lost, like in some sort of pirate attack? Then the airlock would serve as an extra security measure."

"Pirates? In this day and age?" Vincente shook his head. "Yeah, okay, I can see it. Still though..."

"Different times," Shannon said with a shrug. "You should know how much things change without notice."

"Don't need to remind me," Vincente grumbled as he thought back to his ill-fated call, which had started all of this. Had it only been four days?

"I think the cockpit is this way," Jasmine waved a hand.

"A cockpit near the center of the ship?" Vincente asked before he began to chuckle. "Oh, that's beautiful. I'd forgotten about these ships."

"Huh?" Jasmine asked.

"The engineering space is right next to the cockpit area," Vincente explained as he dredged through his memory. "The cargo holds were scattered around it, serving as both extra armor and storage space. It was pretty smart, if you ask me."

"So I'm going the wrong way?" Jasmine asked.

"No," Vincente said. "Just look for an orange-painted door with a black line across the center."

"What? Why?"

"Because that's the old Thai code for no entry," Vincente explained. "If I'm not mistaken, this is an old Thai freighter from Phu Him Pun."

"Phu Him... what?" Shannon asked.

"We know it now as Morathi," Vincente said. "I really should have recognized this ship earlier."

"Oh, them," Shannon snorted. "Their security is top-notch. Hector stays away from them when taking a job because their security force is that good."

"Yeah, so they say," Vincente grinned but said nothing more. He had some fond memories of slipping through their fingers more than once, though – here his thoughts turned dark – one of those times inadvertently led to him being stuck on a planet full of monstrous demons trying to eat him.

"Found the door," Jasmine interrupted them. "Orange with a stripe through it. Fits the description."

"We're right behind you," Shannon said. "About ten seconds– what the hell?"

Vincente stopped and looked at the mercenary who was staring at the floor. Vincente shined a light down and saw that the mercenary had stepped into something black and oily on the deck of the ship. It glistened in the light and dripped from Shannon's boot.

"Ew?" Shannon said as he tried to wipe the stuff off his boot on the metal deck. Unsuccessful, he tried to scrape it off on a small metal lip on the floor.

"Looks like the ship has an oil leak," Vincente decided after a second of inspection.

"Doesn't smell like oil," Shannon complained.

"You coming?" Jasmine asked, impatient.

"Sorry, yeah, on our way," Vincente said and gave Shannon a friendly shove in the back. "C'mon, let's move."

"This shit is sticky," Shannon complained as they moved down the hall. They stopped when they spotted Jasmine fiddling with a door.

It was orange with a stripe through it, just as he had predicted, he saw as he shined his light on it. The door was dogged with a small level, and a small window allowed him to look inside. He shined his light in and flashed the beam around as he inspected the cockpit.

The cockpit was in relatively good shape, he saw immediately. Other than one broken panel, he roughly identified as an old radar, the cockpit had little damage. It was relatively dust-free as well, with the control console easily recognizable. His eyes continued to scan the room until he spotted what he was looking for.

"The nav computer looks intact," he announced. He looked at Jasmine, who had moved to the edge of the door and was now trying to undo the clamps around the latch. "Can you get us in?"

"Faster than Nerd Boy, apparently," she said and slid the latch up. The door opened with a soft squeal of metal-on-metal.

"Hey!" Shannon protested. "Nothing wrong with that."

"I was growing old and grey waiting for you," Jasmine said with a chuckle. "There's something wrong with that."

"C'mon, let's get the data banks and get out of here," Vincente ordered as he stepped into the cockpit. He saw a small passageway leading to the starboard side of the ship, which he figured was the path to engineering. It was eerily dark in the passageway, darker than the rest of the ship. He shined his light around and grunted in satisfaction. "Clock's ticking. Shannon, help me check the nav computers."

The mercenary pulled out a small device from his pocket. He showed the reader to Vincente. "This'll let me check to see if anything's on still them without dragging them back to the Aardvark."

"Hurry up," Vincente said as Shannon extended two cables from the hand-held reader and plugged them into the computer console. After a moment of scanning, he smiled.

"They're a little dated, but good," Shannon announced.

"Uh, Shannon?"

"What, Jasmine?"

"You've got some black crap on your pants," Jasmine said. Vincente glanced down at Shannon's pants. Sure enough, a large patch of black was on his leg. Vincente chuckled.

"Looks like you more than stepped in something," Vincente teased the mercenary. "You were right. It stinks."

Then the patch of black wriggled.

"Holy shit!" Shannon screamed. "I felt that! Get it off! Get it off!"

Jasmine's kukri appeared in her hand and she slapped the black thing with the flat of her blade. It fell to the floor with a sickly plop and started to wriggle back towards his boot – the same boot which had stepped in the oily black tar substance earlier while boarding. The kukri flashed through the air and hacked the black thing on the floor into two pieces. She carefully poked it with the tip and lifted it up into the light.

It was blob-like, Vincente realized as he shifted his flashlight to it. No eyes that he could see, and no legs either. It was covered in a black slime, which looked eerily similar to the oil that Shannon stepped in earlier. Jasmine flipped it back onto the ground and stepped on it, squishing it beneath her boot.

"That was gross," she said.

"Aw, hell," Shannon whined as he looked at his pants. "I got it all over me."

"Hey, guys?" Vincente said as he shined his light down the hall towards where he had guessed engineering was. The darkness was moving. "Guys?"

"Oh, God," Jasmine whispered as more of the small black blobs began to slither into the cockpit. She whipped her kukri through the air and sliced one near the wall in half. It fell and lay on the deck. "Vincente, get those nav chips out!"

"On it," he nodded and popped open the nav computer. He spotted the items he needed quickly enough. The problem was that they were deep under a collection of old cables and two different motherboards. He shined his light over them and saw that there was a bank of them. He swore. "I'm going to need some time."

"Not sure how much time you'll get," Jasmine said as she took aim and fired. A blob exploded in a spray of black ooze and orange guts. More blobs came out of the shadows. "Yeah, you're not getting much time. Hurry your ass up, Vincente!"

"They're small and I have fat fingers!" Vincente called back as he pried the first of five out. He worked as fast as he could without endangering the computer chips.

"Vincente..." Jasmine warned again. She shot two more of the blobs.

"Got them!" Vincente yelled as he pulled the last chip of the nav computer he needed from the bank.

"Extract!" Jasmine shouted and shot a blob, which had gotten too close. "Yolo, be ready. Coming out hot!"

Black ooze spilled out of the blob, but this only slowed it down. More were coming out of the exposed engineering section. Shannon, nearest to the door, was trying to move closer to seal it. There were too many of the blobs, though, and he found himself being pushed back and away from the door.

"I think they're larvae," Jasmine said as she shot the wounded one again.

"Why would there be larvae inside the ship?" Vincente asked as he pulled out his pistol. He aimed at one blob but Jasmine beat him to it, two perfectly placed shots bisecting the blob and creating a small puddle of ooze beneath the corpse.

"Why are there giant, demonic beings stomping around on a planet that doesn't have the ecology or temperature to actually allow for their natural evolution?" Jasmine snapped back. "I stopped asking questions about this damned place a long time ago, boss. Now focus on staying alive."

The trio quickly began to retreat towards the airlock, shooting the random blob as it appeared. No matter how many they shot and killed, however, more poured out of the engineering space. Vincente began to realize that there were simply wasting ammunition as the slide locked open on his pistol. He shook his head, ejected the spent magazine from his pistol, and struggled to grab a second from his belt. He realized that he was still holding the data chips for the nav computers in his hand and pocketed those.

"Let's haul ass!" Jasmine shouted. Vincente holstered his pistol and turned to run to the airlock. He stopped, though, as something large appeared in front of the airlock. Whatever it was that he saw, it was massive and oddly shaped. It was big, far bigger than any of the other blobs had been. A small flame floated in the space before it. Vincente swallowed nervously.

"What the...?" Vincente's voice trailed off.

"Clear a path," came a deep, familiar voice. Vincente cocked his head.

"Yolo?"

The big mercenary stepped into view.

"I found the flamethrower," he said. "And it fits. Now move."

Vincente wasted no time, grabbing Shannon and pulling the confused mercenary aside. Jasmine, recognizing the flamethrower and its user immediately, grinned as she rushed past.

A short burst of flame erupted from the tip of the nozzle as Yolo tested the range. Satisfied, he let loose a long, steady stream of liquid fire into the oncoming horde of blobs. They began to writhe silently on the deck, sizzling and popping under the intense heat. The smell was horrific and nearly caused Vincente to gag.

Yolo was not bothered by the smell, though. He continued to douse the entire hall with the flamethrower, scouring every inch that he could reach. More blobs came out of the dark, and even more died. Yolo was methodical and precise, and after a few minutes, there wasn't a living blob to be seen. He flicked the flamethrower off and looked back at the others.

"I love flamethrowers!" he grinned. "Can I keep it?"

CHAPTER TWELVE

Once they were safely back on board the Aardvark, the group collapsed from exhaustion, save Yolo. The big man took up a protective spot by the side door in case anything else tried to come after them. Vincente was too tired to point out that the forward window was gone, and the still-functioning side door was far from the only place the Kaiju could make a go of getting inside with them, if the creatures really wanted to. Jasmine took the driver's seat and he plopped down in the seat next to her. She punched some buttons on the controls and the Aardvark's blast shield slid down to cover the shattered windshield. Vincente gave an impressed grunt and wondered why he hadn't thought of doing that.

"So what now?" Shannon asked from he sat in the rear of the vehicle. He was still trying to wipe the black, oily residue of the larvae from his pants, and was failing.

"Now we go back to the research ship and get its nav system back up and running," Jasmine answered. "It's time we got the Hell off this planet."

"Kamol's dead," Vincente reminded her. She gave him a dirty look and he shrugged. "You think we can handle getting these old data chips integrated into the military hardware?"

"Not a problem," Shannon piped in. "Most hardware in vessels like our new ship is designed to be integrated with any and all kinds of chips and stuff. Makes it easier to steal information from enemy vessels, you know?" The group stared at him. "I can do it if you and Jasmine can't. Computers are my thing."

"Yolo, check on the wounded," Jasmine ordered as she fired up the Aardvark's engine and got the battle-damaged APC in motion. The gears ground for a moment before shifting, the transmission making odd noises. Jasmine frowned but said nothing, though Vincente recognized the sound as well. They shared a look as the heavy vehicle began to pick up speed. Jasmine turned the wheel and flipped up a virtual sensor display. It allowed her to drive without running into anything large, and though it was far from perfect, it was preferable to being exposed to the horrors of Gorgon IV.

Reluctantly, Yolo shrugged off the flamethrower unit strapped to his back and sat it gingerly on the floor. "Melts is okay!" he called out as he squatted beside him and checked him over before getting up to approach Hector.

"No..." Vincente heard Yolo mutter in a soft, despairing tone. He turned in chair and saw the big mercenary on his knees next to where Hector lay. The mercenary captain didn't appear to be moving.

"He'd dead, isn't he?" Vincente asked.

Yolo nodded slowly before speaking. "He was a good boss. The best." Yolo's fingers curled up to form a fist. The mercenary smashed it into the Aardvark's wall above Hector's rapidly cooling corpse. "It's not fair! He deserved better than this!"

Vincente shot Jasmine a worried glance as Yolo pounded the wall repeatedly in anger.

"He's losing it, isn't he?" Vincente whispered.

"He was gone a long time ago," Jasmine answered, "but he's still useful. If we can just keep him focused."

"I don't see how..."

"Think of a chainsaw," Jasmine said. "Just aim him, pull the cord and let 'er rip."

"Better find something quick," Vincente muttered as he cast a furtive glance back into the rear of the APC. "I think he actually dented the armor."

"Yolo, take a seat! I'm cranking this thing up to max speed!" Jasmine's voice rose as she called back to the mourning mercenary, eyes never leaving the forward sensor display. Driving by sensors alone at her constantly increasing speed was dangerous and required the bulk of her attention.

"It's not fair!" Yolo continued to wail, though he did stop punching the armor of the APC.

"Crap," Vincente muttered, shifting his bulk and moving out of his seat. "I got this. You get us back to that ship!"

Moving out of the small driver's area, Vincente approached Hector slowly and cautiously. Veins on the huge mercenary's arms were clearly visible and sweat ran freely down his face. Vincente wasn't quite certain whether it was actually sweat or tears. He was not about to ask, though.

Nearby, Shannon's eyes darted back and forth between the two men. They were filled with concern and more than a little bit of fear. Vincente knew the look well. He was certain he looked fairly similar at the moment. He tried to put a scowl on his face.

"You heard the lady, Yolo!" Vincente barked in a tone that demanded immediate action. "Take a seat, damn it."

Unfortunately, Yolo reacted in the polar opposite way of what Vincente wanted.

Yolo spun on Vincente, grabbing him by the arms, and lifting him from the Aardvark's floor. He began to shake Vincente, causing the ship captain's innards to move in multiple unpleasant directions at once. Vincente's teeth began to chatter as a massive wave of nausea passed over him.

"Hey!" Vincente shouted, his arms pinned to his sides by Yolo's grip. He swallowed the urge to be sick and tried to put more authority into his voice. "Let go!"

"Screw this! We don't have time!" Shannon yelled as he jerked a syringe from the med-kit that lay near Melts. He popped the plastic lid off the top and sprang at Yolo. The big mercenary saw him coming and planted a fist into Shannon's already-battered face. With a grunt, Shannon staggered backwards. Between the blow from Yolo and the increasing speed of the Aardvark, he lost his balance. Shannon landed on his butt with a solid thud. The syringe he'd held went bouncing away from him as he spat blood and more teeth.

The poor guy is going to have the dental bill from Hell itself if we survive this, Vincente thought as he drew his pistol out of desperation. Yolo turned back towards him and Vincente leveled the gun at Yolo's chest.

"Yolo..." Vincente warned, his voice wavering slightly. His hand – and the gun being held by it – never moved an inch. "Don't make me do this. You really don't want to do this."

"It's not fair!" the big man raged. He took a step towards Vincente.

"Fine," Vincente said and dropped the angle of the gun three feet lower. "It's not fair." He pulled the trigger.

The round tore into Yolo's thigh and exited out the back, a clean through-and-through. Damaged, the leg was unable to support the mercenary. Yolo collapsed onto the floor and began to groan piteously, his hands clutching his thigh. His icy blue eyes met Vincente's brown ones.

"You shot me?"

"The Hell!?" Jasmine shrieked, taking the time to risk a glance over her shoulder at what was transpiring behind her. "You put a bullet in him?"

"It needed to be done," he said calmly as he moved towards where Yolo lay.

"I didn't tell you to shoot him!"

"It worked though, didn't it?" Vincente snapped. "He's down, and it was merely a flesh wound. At worst, it's going to leave a nasty scar, and as tough as he is, it might not even do that much!"

Shannon crawled over, retrieving the syringe on his way, and injected its contents into the side of Yolo's neck. He paused halfway, checked Yolo's heart rate, and decided a little more was in order. He pushed the rest of the sedative in. "And he won't be getting up anytime soon."

"That's just great, guys!" Jasmine complained. "Now we've got four bodies to carry, and there's only three of us."

"I had a damn-near seven foot tall psychotic monster of a man having a mental breakdown back here and you're complaining about how I kept myself alive?" Vincente asked as he threw his hands up into the air. "Your priorities, woman, are seven different kinds of screwed up."

"He's got a point," Shannon offered.

"You need to shut the Hell up, or I will do it for you," Jasmine warned. Shannon wisely shut his mouth. "Boss, how're we going to get them onto the ship when we get there? That Kaiju... Kage? He could still be in there!"

"We'll figure it out!" Vincente yelled back, his temper fraying. "We'll figure it out, like we always do. We'll leave them here, and–"

"We shouldn't leave any of them!" Jasmine screamed back. "We're better than that!"

"So then what? We go aboard, carrying them, and then die?" Vincente asked, unable to keep the sarcasm out of his tone any longer. "We leave them on the Aardvark, where they'll be safe, and come back for them after we kill that thing!"

"Oh," Jasmine said as she visibly deflated. "I thought..."

"I know what you thought," Vincente said. "You know me better than that. At least, I thought you did."

"That's a cheap shot," Jasmine snapped back. "Today has not been a good one, okay? You sounded like you were just going to leave Yolo and Melts here to die."

"You shot me..." a groggy voice sounded from beneath Vincente's feet.

"I thought you said he'd be out for awhile?" Vincente asked the small mercenary. Shannon shrugged his shoulders.

"That dosage should have knocked out a horse," Shannon observed.

"Whatever," Vincente shook his head. He glanced down at Yolo. "Hey big guy, calm down yet?"

"Vincente, get up here and take over for a moment," Jasmine called out. "Let me handle this."

Vincente went back to the front, and after letting Jasmine slide past him, plopped down into the driver's seat of the Aardvark. The vehicle slowed momentarily when Jasmine moved, but as soon as Vincente was in place, it started to pick up speed again as his foot found the accelerator, though it did not move at nearly the same clip that Jasmine had pushed it to. Vincente was cautious, and not nearly experienced enough in any sort of sensor-only driving to risk going faster.

Jasmine dropped to her knees next to Yolo, who was trying to pick himself up off the floor. Jasmine pushed his chest back and inspected the wound. After a second, she was nodding. Though her captain had shot the man, his aim had been true. More than likely, there wouldn't be any lasting damage to the muscle tissue in Yolo's leg. More importantly, it meant that he would probably be able to walk soon if they pumped a few stims into him.

"Hey, you're okay," she told him. "Yolo, you're okay."

Yolo was looking over her shoulder with murder in his eyes. "That bastard shot me!"

"Forget him, Yolo," she purred and bent over to place her lips on the giant's. Yolo struggled for a moment then gave into the kiss. When Jasmine lifted her head and their lips parted, Yolo was motionless beneath her with a dumbfounded expression on his face.

"I love you," he said.

"You're adorable and you're wounded," she said as she grabbed the med-kit. She dug through it for a moment before finding what she needed to fix his leg temporarily. Antiseptic in hand, she cut a small square in the clothing around the bullet hole in his leg before dousing it liberally. As his eyes widened as the high-alcohol content disinfectant hit his nerves, she smiled and winked at him before turning her attention back to his gunshot wound.

"Heh," Yolo chuckled as Jasmine slapped a pressure bandage over the oozing, bleeding hole. Jasmine glanced up from her work and looked at the mercenary.

"What's so funny?" she asked as applied another bandage to the exit hole on the other side of his leg. Satisfied, she wiped her hands on her pants. "You should be in some pain. A lot of pain, actually."

"I got to see your boobs," he said, pride evident in his tone. Jasmine rolled her eyes.

"Seriously? Now you can't die on this misbegotten planet."

"Why not?"

"Because I'm going to kick your ass once you're healed."

"You do like me," Yolo said, then groaned as Jasmine pushed on the bandage. He grimaced. "Maybe."

"I like skinny guys," Jasmine said. "Delicate things, you know? Doesn't threaten their masculinity when I kick their ass. By the time they get to me, they're used to it. Plus, I like to be in control in bed. You're an Alpha type. Won't work."

"You're amazing," Yolo said. He looked over the bandage and grunted. "Looks good. I think I'll live."

"Now quit trying to get me to take your clothes off and focus on getting off this damn world alive, okay?"

"Okay."

"And no killing Vincente, either," she warned.

"Oh, come on! He shot me!" the big man protested.

"Flesh wound," she reminded him.

"So... are you still crazy?" Shannon asked in a meek voice.

"That's rude," Yolo said. "I just got weird for a moment. Forgot myself. Let the rage grow until I couldn't control it anymore."

"So... controlled crazy?"

"He's fine, Shannon," Jasmine said, exasperated.

"Jasmine," Vincente called from the front of the Aardvark. "You're not going to believe this."

"Now what?" she asked.

"I think we're lost."

"How can we be lost?" she demanded as she left Yolo's side and moved to the front. She leaned on the driver's seat and jabbed a finger at the small map on the console. "See that glowing red thing? That's us. The glowing blue thing? That's our destination. How can you be 'lost'?"

"Where'd all this yellow squiggly stuff come from?"

"What?" she asked and looked closer at the digital map. She blinked. "Lower the blast shield."

"Oooookay," Vincente drawled slowly and pressed in the command.

The dark shield quickly rose and disappeared into the crevice above the shattered remnants of the windshield. Neither of them noticed the small piece of safety glass, which fell onto the console, nor did they hear the whine of the servo motor as it struggled with the weight of the shield. Their attention was fixated solely on their surroundings.

"That," Vincente whistled softly, "is something we should have known about."

That was a massive building set in the middle of their path, blocking the only navigable way through the narrow pass. The stone building – it resembled a temple to Vincente, though he could not put his finger on any particular reason – had elaborate carvings in the stonework. A large entrance, almost as high as the sides of the ravine, was the only apparent way into the building. A shimmering blue field blocked the entrance, a gate if Vincente had ever seen one. On either side of the gate stood tall, cragged faces of a cliff, insurmountable obstacles that looked to be over one hundred feet high.

"I think it's a temple of some sort," he whispered under his breath. "Or the most oddly placed fortress in the history of mankind."

"That's Zubulun," Jasmine hissed. "Looks like it's inhabited, too."

"You think the military knew it was here?" He asked her. She shook her head.

"They wouldn't have dared try to land on a Zubulun planet," she countered.

"So... what do we do?"

"Back up and try to get out of here without being noticed?" Jasmine suggested.

"Too late for that," Vincente jerked his chin at the gate. Multiple guards had come out, their weapons trained on the Aardvark. Larger turrets appeared from behind cleverly disguised rocks and holes in the cliff faces, their barrels points directly at the driver's compartment of the APC. A faint hum filled the air, telling the two of them just how powered and ready the fort's weaponry was. "I think we've been made."

"Would you kindly exit your vehicle, sans weaponry, and wait to be escorted inside? Failure to comply with our instructions will necessitate a quick demise for all parties on board," a voice called out from the fort.

Jasmine sighed. "Zubuluns. They may kill us, but at least they'll be polite about it."

INTERLUDE V

"Did you know that there is a growing belief among the most classicist branch of religion ideology that the Zubuluns are one of the reputed Lost Tribes of Israel?" Professor Hans Jurgen asked theoretically, as he leaned back in his seat. Across from him, the Prosecutor blinked slowly, roused from a sleep-like state, which had settled over him sometime during the past hour during Jurgen's boring lecture.

"Zubulun?" the Prosecutor asked, his brain waking at the name of the strongest military power in the space near the Gorgon star. He flipped back through his screen and read some notes. "You mentioned the planet, but never the Zubuluns. Do you know any secrets which may help the military in case of any potential war with them at a later date?"

"Of course not," the professor scoffed. "The very notion that these... people descend from Abraham's children is rather absurd. They merely took the name and that's it."

"What do you know of them, professor?" the Prosecutor yawned sleepily and rested his elbows on the table between them. "Excuse me. It's just that it's been a long time since college."

"Understandable," Jurgen smiled. "The Zubulun, according to their own mythology and what I've seen in the public forum, like to think of themselves as the lost military tribe of Jerusalem. Like the Bene Israel of India, but with a decidedly more militaristic approach to their everyday lives. Truth be told, it's common knowledge in my community – that's the factual, scientific one – that the Zubuluns are nothing more than a bunch of hopped up colonial monarchists from the old United Kingdom."

"Isn't that where Oxford is located?" the Prosecutor asked, interested at last in what the professor was talking about.

The professor chuckled. "Dear me, no. Oxford is located on Earth."

"Uh..." the Prosecutor paused for a moment, clearing his head. "You're telling me that Oxford is not in the United Kingdom?"

"The United Kingdom ceased to be a functioning government hundreds of years ago," the professor answered in a smug tone.

"That would be like claiming that Earth United's capitol is located in Piscataway territory."

"Who?"

"The Piscataway? Indian tribe formerly located in the Chesapeake Bay area in Norte Americana?"

"I'd never heard of them," the Prosecutor admitted.

"An indigenous tribe of natives from the area, before overly aggressive Pax Europa colonization of the land began were descended from the Algonquin tribes further to the north–"

"Fascinating and all," the Prosecutor interrupted. "But what else can you tell me about the Zubulun?"

"As I said," Jurgen sniffed and smoothed down his hair with his hands. "They are monarchists. Such a dreadful political entity, monarchy. The absolute rule of a king or queen stifles the growth of a people both intellectually and metaphysically. How can the people share in the suffering if one person rules above all else? No, the lack of a class system in a monarchist state is against the very ethos and nature that man has designed for himself."

"That... made no sense to me at all," the Prosecutor admitted.

"Of course, it doesn't," Jurgen smiled and rapped the table with his knuckles. "You are not an enlightened man."

CHAPTER THIRTEEN

"Your wounded shall be cared for, as will your dead," their guard said in an almost apologetic tone as he ushered the four into a large holding cell deep within the walled fortress. "We do regret this necessity, but until we have a chance to ascertain why you and your crew are here, captain, we must keep you in custody. You do understand our position, correct?"

"Yeah, thanks," Vincente nodded as the group filed into the small cell. He looked around and spotted bunks off to the side, and toiletries already prepared for them. There was a decided lack of bars on the sole window of the cell. If Vincente didn't know better, he would have sworn that he had been put up in a protected guest suite and not a jail cell. "Nice digs."

"We are an outpost on the edge of reality and the unknown," the guard said with a slight shrug. "It is unbecoming to force anyone – guests or permanent residents – to reside in horrific conditions."

"Thank you," Jasmine said with a bright smile. "These are far better quarters than I imagined we would get for accidentally trespassing on your land."

"Oh, this isn't our land, milady," the guard said as he closed the door to the cell. He locked the door. "It was never our land."

Vincente listened as the guard walked away, confused. He had been lured to this world on false pretenses, and now everything he thought he knew had flown out the window. The Zubulun guard actually sounded sorry that he had been ordered to lock them up. Zubulun politeness, while normal, had actually seemed a bit over-the-top to the captain.

Vincente inspected the walls and ceiling of the cell. It was obviously a new construction, one that the Hegemony had put a lot of effort into constructing and decorating to maximize the comfort of anyone in the cell. It even featured a private shower, complete with privacy screen. He walked over to the sink and tested it. He grunted. Hot water.

"This is a damn strange turn of events," Vincente observed as he turned off the water.

"Tell me about it," Jasmine said as she eyed the door. "It's sturdy, but look... it's designed to resist impacts from the outside and not in. If Yolo got a running start, he'd probably bring the door down easily enough."

"I'm not running anywhere," the big mercenary grumbled. "Some asshole shot me."

"Holy crap! Let it go, merc," Vincente said. "It was just a flesh wound."

"Fine," Yolo nodded. "Next time, I give you a flesh wound."

"Boys," Jasmine warned, "play nice." Both Vincente and Yolo shut up.

"This is the nicest jail I've ever seen," Shannon agreed once the two bigger men quit arguing. "Beds for everyone."

"These walls are reinforced, but I can't shake the feeling that... this is a defensive position, not a jail or temple of any kind," Jasmine decided as she continued to inspect their surroundings. "Now why in the universe would the Hegemony need a defensive position on a planet that is on the edge of their space?"

"Figures," Vincente complained as he flopped down onto one of the bunks. "They'd stake a nice prison right in the middle of a planet infested with Kaiju."

"That's stupid," Jasmine argued. "If they wanted a prison, they'd put it somewhere else. Are you even listening to me, Vincente?"

"Stupid aristocratic..." Vincente's mutterings trailed off as he closed his eyes. "Sheets. Nice."

"No, you're not listening," Jasmine sighed.

"High thread count," Vincente said as his fingertips gently traced a circular pattern on the bed sheet. "Is this... Egyptian cotton?"

"Someone's coming," Jasmine said as she pressed her ear against the door. "Four people, sounds like. That was quick."

"That doesn't bode well," Vincente said as he sat up in the bed. He sighed. "I really could use a nap."

"I could use a shower," Jasmine admitted as the lock on the door clicked. A moment later, a tall thin man walked into the room. Thinning white hair covered his head, and a neatly trimmed white beard adorned his face. Over his left eye, he wore a patch. In the grey and green uniform of the Hegemony, he appeared to be nothing more than another Zubulun officer. The newcomer looked each of them over, his good eye sparkling in the light.

Vincente squinted. "You know, from the right angle, you kinda look like–"

"Captain Mbunti Dandridge!" Jasmine nearly squealed. "Hero of Vesper! Defender of Io!"

"Didn't you die?" Vincente asked, surprised.

"He was lost during a mission to Gorgon IV, defending... wait," Jasmine paused in her excited explanation as everything began to sink in. She struggled to put the pieces together. "You were lost here, fighting the Zubulun. Why are you wearing their uniform?"

"I hope you find your accommodations adequate," Dandridge said, his voice a rich and deep baritone. "We're not used to having guests here. Even the kind we have to... lock up, for the time being."

"I don't understand..." Jasmine said.

"This planet – these people – I thought were the enemy for so long? Well, they're not. Not quite, at least," Dandridge informed her. "We have a few minutes of time before I have to bring you to the base commander, so I can explain it to you on our way."

"I suppose," Vincente said as he rolled off the bunk. "We'll have to go slow. We have a walking wounded."

"Because of you," Yolo growled.

"Okay, I'm sorry," Vincente heaved a mighty sigh. "Never happen again. I swear."

"Good," Yolo nodded.

"If you will?" Dandridge motioned for the group to follow. As they fell into step next to him, the other three men – guards, as Jasmine had predicted – fell in behind them, though their guns weren't pointed at their backs. Not quite, at least. As they walked down the hallway, Dandridge began to speak.

"I was on the Gnarler, as you well know, and I was part of Task Force Orion. We were on a mission to repel the Zubulun spearhead, namely to stop them before they claimed the Gorgon system. However, unbeknownst to my crew or me, one of the other ships in our task force – the Lysacles, if you are curious – had a very different set of orders. Orders I was not made aware of until much later.

"Ah, but that comes later. Our fifteen ship task force would normally have been more than enough to stop any Zubulun group. Fifteen Hydra-class battleships? The entire Zubulun Fourth Fleet couldn't have matched that at the time. We had to show them we were serious, and while it deprived us of our defensive screen from the Morathi, it was worth the risk.

"So there we were, the most powerful task force ever assembled, moving in on the Zubulun fleet, their cowardly ships not daring to fire upon us as we moved closer. We grew cocky, arrogant. They weren't willing to fight. They'd reached the end of the rope. They were terrified of our massive manhood. They would celebrate our 'liberating' of their enslaved selves and join our noble cause.

"Don't roll your eyes. That was one of the tamer theories I heard while standing on my ship's bridge. But just as we hailed them to demand their surrender, the Lysacles suddenly dove for the surface of one of the planets in the Gorgon system. Gorgon IV, as it turned out. The previously timid and meek Zubulun suddenly came alive and began to fire upon the Lysacles, destroying it in such a barrage of firepower that it caught all of us off guard.

"We didn't know what to do. We'd been expecting a fight, true. But the pure ferocity of it... was something one had to see with their own eyes. We turned our fire on the Zubulun fleet and returned it in kind. Over the next five hours, the space around Gorgon IV was filled with ejected plasma, debris from dozens of ships, and thousands of bodies. It was complete and absolute carnage, something I had not seen in a very long time.

"My ship went down on Gorgon IV. It was later, when I was rescued by the same people who I'd been fighting previously with, when I learned of the massive creatures who inhabited this planet and the Zubulun commitment to keeping them here on the planet, and not out amongst the stars."

"So this is a fort," Jasmine breathed.

"Of course," Dandridge nodded and smiled. His white teeth gleamed against dark skin. "What did you think this was, some sort of temple?"

"Er..." Vincente mumbled. "No?"

"By the way, we greatly appreciate the effort you took to kill off that many of the beings," Dandridge stated. "Nuking them? I wish we'd have thought of that."

"I'm sorry, but why don't you kill them all?" Jasmine asked as they began to climb a set of stairs. Small, dim lighting lit their way, and while there was plenty of natural light to see by, courtesy of overhead windows, the lights were a comfort. "You have the means. I've seen the Zubulun fight."

"Ah, well, that's an ethical argument I'm not prepared to get into at this time," Dandridge explained. "Just try to remember that Zubulun, unlike United Earth, values all life. Even the kind which is constantly trying to eat his face off."

"Values all life?" Yolo snorted through his nose.

"Values, yes," Dandridge smiled. "Still willing to kill something or someone who is threatening them, however. Do not mistake a lack of desirability to kill as an unwillingness to do what is needed, which for the Zubulun – and now me as well – means doing everything in its power to keep this planet contained."

"So we're not ever allowed to leave?" Jasmine asked, her tone carefully neutral.

Dandridge looked at her and smiled. "Don't be ridiculous. We want you gone to spread the word about how dangerous this planet is. We just aren't letting you go without inspecting your ship for any sign of the creatures. Call it our own private and personal assurance."

"We've been calling them 'Kaiju', actually," Vincente breathed, secretly relieved. He had seen the familiar tension in Jasmine's shoulders and had been dreading a fight in the narrow corridor. He had not liked his odds of surviving.

"Huh... fitting, actually," Dandridge nodded. "These are strange creatures indeed. Terrible creatures. The Zubulun weren't sure whether these were demonic beings sent by God to punish man for his transgressions, or something darker, older than the battle in Heaven itself. Either way, they took it as their solemn duty to protect mankind from these creatures, even if the rest of mankind believes that the Zubulun have ulterior motives. Ah, here we are."

They had stopped before a plain door at the end of the long hallway. Two Zubulun guards stood at either side of the door, their eyes scanning the newcomers with a combination of suspicion and curiosity. Suspicion, because Vincente knew that the Zubulun were naturally suspicious of everyone. The curiosity was a bit confusing, though. He asked about it and Dandridge laughed loudly.

"These are boys who have been on rotation here for almost eleven standard months now," Dandridge said. He made a small motion with his hand towards Jasmine. "This is the first woman they're seen since leaving home. Probably not sure what to make of you, Miss."

"Boys," Jasmine said with a shake of her head. "Staff Sergeant Jasmine Alandé, formerly of the Defense Corps. Keep your hands to yourself if you want to keep them attached to your wrists."

Dandridge chuckled as both guards abruptly averted their eyes. "Ah, the wonders of a reputation."

The door opened and another man in uniform showed them inside. Another man in uniform and wearing a colonel's rank sat behind the desk in the office. The walls were mostly unadorned, except for a solitary plaque on the wall behind him. Dandridge closed the door behind Shannon once they were all inside. The three other guards who had followed them from their cell waited outside the room, which struck Vincente as odd. He wasn't sure what was going on around here, but it wasn't entirely in line with what he knew of the Zubulun.

Then again, he listened to the same propaganda vids that everyone else did.

"Sir," Dandridge said and came to attention. Jasmine followed suit, though Vincente lazily waved. Yolo and Shannon stood slightly behind him, shifting from one foot to the other, and uncertainty on both of their faces. Dandridge continued.

"Please make yourselves comfortable," the colonel said and motioned for them to sit. Vincente glanced around and spotted a few chairs, which had already been brought into the room. He grabbed one before anyone else could and sat down. The others followed his lead, and in a moment, everyone was listening intently to what the Zubulun base commander was saying.

"First off, I am not going to kill any of you," he began as he lit a cigar. "That is most definitely not in my nature. I would like to think of myself as a protector of man, and not a murderer of one. So you have no reason to fear me or my men.

"Secondly, you must understand that we have no desire to keep you here indefinitely," the commander repeated what Dandridge had told them before. "I presume that you have a way off planet, and all that we ask is that you do not take with you any of these creatures off the planet. To ensure this, we will be sending a marine platoon to escort you to your vessel. They will provide both external security, as well as assist with your departure from this planet.

"If you are found in possession of any creature which is a natural denizen of this planet, your vessel will be interred and you shall be summarily executed in accordance to our laws. Do you understand?"

"I do, yes," Vincente shifted in his seat. "I should tell you, though, that our, ah, ship is really a former United Earth ship we kinda salvaged when our own ship was destroyed in a nuclear explosion."

"That was a truly impressive feat," the commander nodded.

"I should also tell you that the United Earth ship was designed to transport one of the Kaiju – that's what we call your creatures – off-world, and they entire crew was killed by something on board," Vincente continued in a rush, his palms sweating nervously as the commander eyed him. "The Kaiju might still be on board the ship."

"I... see," the commander nodded. He looked over at Dandridge. "Mbunti, as much as I would love to send you with them, I believe that Captain Duvall will have a better grasp of the fluidity of the situation there, having been here for longer." Seeing Vincente's confusion, he explained. "Captain Gina Duvall, earner of two Medals of Valor, both the Bronze and Silver. She is in charge of security and threat assessment here. She also is the toughest and most intelligent marine I have ever met."

"Ah, thank you, but–" Vincente began, but the base commander cut him off.

"I know that you expected – even hoped for – Mbunti to escort you, but trust me, you could be in no finer hands than those of Captain Duvall."

"Thank you, sir," Jasmine said, overriding Vincente's coming protest.

"As an added bonus, I already have the marines ready and waiting to escort you and your crew to your new vessel, Captain Huerta," the commander nodded. "Thank you for being patient with us."

"I... ah... no, thank you," Vincente exhaled slowly, confused. "I just..."

"Expected something else?" here the commander chuckled. "You are not out of the woods yet, as the expression goes. Captain Duvall will escort you with haste to your ship. It is your responsibility to get it off the ground and to ensure that it is clear of any of the creatures. I expect you to accept your responsibility with all the seriousness that it must entail."

"We will," Vincente promised. "We were tricked into coming here, and just want to leave. The problem is that United Earth will be looking for us, and they'll be looking for us with murder on their mind."

"Let me see if I can put in a few calls to my government," the commander suggested. "Dandridge is a prime example of former Earthers joining our cause, but not the only one."

"No offense, sir, but if I ever see this planet again, it'll be too soon," Vincente stated.

"Well, I can authorize passports on my own," the commander mulled the idea over before coming to a decision. "Yes, yes. Passports, Zubulun passports, will do nicely. Nobody will question you too closely, as long as you stay away from any of the United Earth-controlled planets. Fringe worlds; wild, but some luxurious resorts out that way. Those would be a wonderful hiding place, especially if one had the financial capital to stay there indefinitely. Do you think you can manage that, captain?"

"I don't get it," Vincente frowned. "Why would you do this? I don't see what you get out of this."

"We have our reasons," Dandridge said. Vincente shook his head angrily.

"I'm not buying that."

"Then buy this. The creatures, the Kaiju are a danger to the entire galaxy. The EU government wants to take one of the intelligent ones off-world to weaponize," Dandridge said in a flat, dangerous voice. "You need to hide from them, because you know the truth. We want you off this planet, because we have no desire to see you harmed. Lastly, you are enhancing the reputation of this planet by disappearing. You are notorious, from what I hear. Famed captain disappears after working on a secret transport for the EU government? Nobody is going to want to come here now."

"Plus, we will take that research vessel of theirs off your hands at market value," the commander added. "Market value, captain. That is close to seven billion credits, give or take."

"Captain," Jasmine pleaded. "This is that chance. Remember when I told you we need to stop, take one last job and retire to some luxury world and get body sculpts? This is it. Dandridge is an honorable man, I know this with all of my soul. He'd have made one hell of a Corps officer."

"So Captain Huerta, what shall it be?"

"Yes sir, I think I will take your offer," Vincente smiled at last. "A few billion credits sounds good to me."

"Excellent then! Let us get you on your way, and I shall have your passports waiting for you at Wales. Is this acceptable?"

"Yes sir," Vincente nodded.

"Now come. Time for you to meet my marines."

****

"My name is Captain Gina Duvall," the strong faced woman said as she stuck out her hand to Vincente. The captain shook it, and then winced as she squeezed it slightly. She frowned but said nothing as she cast an eye over the group. Shannon tried to hide behind Yolo, who was still looking emotionally stable but ready to go. Vincente had multiple small scratches on his face, much to his annoyance. Only Jasmine appeared to be fully functioning and unharmed, though her armor was stained with Kaiju blood.

"Nice to meet you, ma'am," Vincente said, terrified of the woman. She reminded him a lot of Moony back when they were younger. Such a forceful personality on that one.

"We have five APCs tasked to escort your Aardvark to your ship," she continued after a moment. "Once there, I will escort you to your ship to ensure that the hold and the environment is clear. Once this occurs, you will be cleared for launch and proceed to the planet of Wales."

"We really appreciate it," Vincente said. Captain Duvall nodded her head and looked back at the assembled marines behind her. "Company, mount up!"

The Zubulun marines, their camouflage uniforms blending perfectly with the scrub-like desert around the fort, boarded their APCs while Jasmine hopped into the driver's compartment of the Aardvark. After some initial reluctance, Shannon took the turret while Vincente and Yolo each took a gun port.

They exited out the rear gate of the fort with two of the heavy Zubulun APCs leading the way. The group fanned out a little bit as they picked up speed, the Earther spaceship a mere twenty minutes from the fortress. Dandridge had been rather shocked at that revelation. There was supposed to be a fleet orbiting Gorgon IV, both protecting the planet and preventing from any accidental landings. Neither Dandridge nor the base commander had any idea where the fleet had gone, and this caused some consternation.

Not my problem, Vincente thought as his eyes adjusted to the painfully bright sunlight. I just need to get off this damned planet before anyone else dies.

The APCs rumbled along. The air outside the Aardvark was breezy, cooler than previous, signifying that the sun was finally setting on the hellish world. Vincente felt himself growing sleepy as the gentle, rhythmic rocking of the APC lulled him into a sense of security. He felt his eyes grow heavy and he kept dozing off.

The APC stopped. Vincente jerked his head up.

"I wasn't asleep!" he insisted. He blinked his eyes and looked out the gun port. "Where are we?"

"I think we're here," Yolo said. He pounded a fist on the roof. "Yo, Shannon! We got anything?"

"I'm wearing a radio, you twit," Shannon said over the comm. "And yes, we're here."

"Awesome," Yolo grunted. "Smooth ride. That was easy. Easy sailing from here."

"Oh, hell," Vincente muttered under his breath. "We're hosed."

"Contact!" came the call from above. Unsurprising, Vincente thought.

Something heavy crashed into the side of the stopped APC. Metal squealed as the heavy object kept pushing into their side. Shannon started screaming out as the pushing continued, unintelligible at first but growing steadily understandable as the moments wore on.

"Captain Duvall! Your APC just rammed us!" Vincente heard Jasmine call out over the comm. "Captain!"

"Our driver was just decapitated by something," Duvall reported a moment later. "Please stand by as we regain control of our vehicle."

"Polite," Vincente mused. "Yolo, with me. Let's get out of here before we get crushed by our allies."

Vincente leaned over and pushed open the rear door of the Aardvark. He popped his head out and looked around.

The ground was littered with small, strange Kaiju, the likes of which he had never imagined seeing before. Shapeless and black, with long spears sticking out at random locations all over their blob-like bodies, they were the very embodiment of unknown terror. One of the Zubulun marines got too close to one, and a ten foot spear shot out of the body and impaled the marine. His painful screams were drowned out as the spear began to shift form, invading the man's body as it drove upwards and onwards. The marine began to twitch randomly as his neural center was violently taken over by the Kaiju. The marine fell, dead before he hit the ground. A moment later the spear fell out of the body and turned into a black puddle, reforming with the Kaiju which had thrown it. He blinked in surprise as the massive guns on each of the Zubulun APCs began to fire into the seething mass of Kaiju, startling him out of his reverie. He frowned and, after a moment of hesitation, pulled his head back inside to the relative safety of the APC and slammed the rear door shut.

"Nope."

"Vincente!" Jasmine fairly screamed at him from the front of the Aardvark. "Get your fat ass out there so we can get off this world!"

"Damn it," Vincente muttered. Yolo grabbed his giant sniper rifle and looked at him. Vincente sighed and picked up one of Hector's smaller carbines. The mercenary captain, who had been buried back at the Zubulun fort, would not complain, Vincente figured. "Okay, let's go out there and probably die."

"That's the spirit!" Yolo shouted and thumped him on the back.

"Yay." Vincente pushed the back door open again and hopped out. He aimed and shot one little Kaiju that had gotten a bit too close for his comfort. He looked up at the research vessel he was stealing – salvaging, he mentally reminded himself – and the hair on the back of his neck rose. Something about the ship has set off a subconscious warning, but for the life of him he did not know what that warning was.

The Zubulun APC had regained control and was no longer trying to destroy his Aardvark, he saw. Atop the Aardvark, Shannon was opening up into a particularly large cluster of Kaiju, spent ammunition casings scattering around the APC. Jasmine has exited the Aardvark as well, her massive hand cannon – a gift from her last commanding officer, Vincente recalled – out of its holster.

The turret above the Aardvark suddenly ceased firing. Confused, Vincente looked up to see why Shannon had quit shooting. He gagged as the shredded body of Shannon fell limply into the turret's seat. He turned away quickly, trying to keep the rising gorge down. He hadn't liked the short mercenary as much as he had like his leader, but no man deserved to die that way. He turned his head back as Yolo cried out in pain.

Four of the small Kaiju had attacked Yolo, slashing him and knocking him to the ground. The huge mercenary fought valiantly, but the shape shifting Kaiju were too much and Yolo quickly disappeared into the inky blackness. More swarmed him, and he couldn't hear the mercenary's cries any more. Vincente sighed and began to shoot some of the Kaiju who were looking to join in on the attack.

Crazy, but one hell of a warrior, Vincente thought as he wrote off the giant.

Suddenly, Jasmine was there, dancing between the Kaiju, slashing and slicing every single Kaiju within range of her Kukri. The Kaiju pulled themselves off the large mercenary and struggled to stop the one-woman killing machine that Jasmine had changed into. They flung their black spears at her, tried to stab her, slow her down, trip her, something, anything to stop this whirling dervish of madness and lethality.

The Kaiju failed. Miserably.

As Jasmine finished beheading the final Kaiju, which had tried to attack her, Vincente was slammed into the Aardvark. Something had struck him in the back, and while his armor had protected him, it had still hurt. He spun and fired a quick burst into the Kaiju that had attacked him. The little beast flopped into the dirt, dead. His eyes lifted back to the ship and saw that the Kaiju horde was beginning to thin out.

"Can someone lay down some damn cover fire?" Vincente shouted as he pressed his body against the Aardvark's body. He cast a worried glance over at Jasmine, but the diminutive pilot had already commandeered Yolo's large caliber hunting rifle. He looked over at the thrice-wounded mercenary and grimaced. From his position, it appeared that the body armor, which the large man wore, had not been enough to stop the blade-like arms of the smaller Kaiju. Blood flowed freely from the nasty gouges in his chest and stomach. Vincente was almost happy that the mercenary was unconscious, and unable to see his guts flopping about.

"Captain, you need to get off my planet," Duvall's squad moved away from the Aardvark and back to their own transports. "Get your ass onto that ship!"

"I haven't cleared it yet!" Vincente howled, frustrated at the Zubulun captain. He found himself wishing, not for the first time that Dandridge had been tasked to guide the remnants of his crew to the research vessel and not the hard-nosed, stubborn Marine. He peeked over the engine compartment hood and saw that the

Zubulun APC was clearing a path for him, the 57mm machine gun destroying the Kaiju with relative ease.

"Boss!" Jasmine cried out. Vincente looked up and saw that a solitary Kaiju had made it to the top of the Aardvark while he had been distracted. The evil little thing hissed and its tongue lashed out at him. The serrated edge slashed his cheek and drew blood. Vincente cried out in pain and fell back, trying to target the Kaiju with his rifle. He fired twice and both rounds, poorly aimed, flew off into the yonder. The Kaiju hissed again and leapt into the air, claws extended as it aimed for him face.

Time seemed to slow for Vincente as razor-sharp claws punctured through his armor and pierced his shoulder. Pain filled his body and his mind clouded as every nerve in his body seemed to be on fire. More pained erupted in his other shoulder and he felt, dimly, a part of his shoulder being eaten. His eyes clenched shut as he waited for his death.

A loud roar filled his ears. A warm rain coated his face. A vile taste filled his mouth, and for a moment, the pain subsided as he gagged on the horrid and putrid liquid. He opened his eyes and saw that the Kaiju was gone. Leaning over him was Jasmine, the smoking barrel of her sniper rifle clearly evident. She had a worried look on her face.

"Oh damn, boss," she whispered as she surveyed his wounds. He tried to smile but with the purple and black blood of the Kaiju on his face, it looked more like a grimace than anything. Which it probably does look like, he allowed as the pain came roaring back. He groaned as parts of him that he didn't know could hurt began to.

"Hurts," he hissed through clenched teeth. "Kaiju... poisoned?"

"Maybe, I don't know," she admitted as she began to administer first aid. "The Zubulun have cleared a path to the ship and that bitchy captain of theirs, Duvall, got Yolo on board."

"Haven't cleared..." he tried. "Kage."

"Don't worry about it, boss," she said, tears in her eyes. She slapped on a pressure bandage and injected him with a painkiller, then placed another pressure bandage on the other puncture wound. He tried to sit up, but a sudden and inexplicable wave of euphoria washed over him. He no longer wanted to sit up. Now, he just wanted to sleep, maybe daydream a little, which was odd, because he knew he needed to do something very important but for the life of him, he could not remember what it was. He looked at Jasmine, who was still looking down at him.

"Best. Employee. Ever."

"Captain Duvall – you know, Gina? The Marine Captain from Hell? She is going to have some of her Marines watch over you while we take a squad and clear the ship," Jasmine told him. "Be a good captain and don't die on me now, okay?"

She patted him on his uninjured cheek, rested her commandeered sniper rifle against the Aardvark and stood up. She squared her shoulders and looked at the research vessel as Duvall slowly approached. The Marine's body armor was covered with the black and purple ichors of the Kaiju.

"There's power in that ship," Duvall said. "Why does that ship have power?"

"Kage is inviting us in," Jasmine said. "The one that you call the Darkness."

"Oh, holy balls," Duvall muttered and crossed herself. Twice. "We try to avoid that one."

"No avoiding him this time," Jasmine shook her head and sighed. "We have to keep them on this planet, but since that's our only ride off here–"

"Only because our next ship won't come for five more months," Duvall reminded her.

"Right," Jasmine nodded. She checked her handgun and saw that she had only two magazines left, plus the eight rounds in the current and loaded one. Twenty-eight rounds. "That should be enough. Maybe."

"I've got fifteen wounded, four KIA," Duvall said. "I think it's just going to be us girls on this one. I need to leave a squad out here to cover their flanks. My APC gunners are good, but our turret speed is slow compared to your Aardvark's."

"Yeah, but yours is armored and protected," Jasmine reminded her as she looked up at the dangling mess that had been Shannon still locked into the Aardvark's turret. The mercenary almost looked peaceful up there, dead and cooling in the late afternoon sun. Or would have, had his face not been ripped off by a marauding Kaiju.

She sighed. Life really wasn't fair sometimes. She looked at the Marine captain, a practically unknown in her book. She glanced back at the research vessel, which looked warm and inviting. Near the entrance to the airlock lay Yolo, guarded by three of the Zubulun marines. His guts had been pushed back into his stomach, though the possibility of a punctured bowel meant that he'd probably be dead within twenty-four hours unless she got him to an emergency care facility off-planet. He was conscious, though he was in a lot of pain and would be better off asleep, she knew from past experience.

Life wasn't fair. Life, it seemed, actually sucked. Fine. So be it. She double-checked the chamber of her handgun and touched the kukri still strapped to her chest. She was as ready as she ever would be.

"Let's go," Jasmine said.

CHAPTER FOURTEEN

Jasmine left the door of the spaceship open once they were situated inside.

"In case we want to get out of here in a hurry," Jasmine told the confused marine. Understanding flashed across Duvall's eyes and she nodded in agreement.

"So where do we start?" Duvall asked. She pulled back the charge handle of her carbine and looked around. "Nice ship. Looks military."

"It was, before we, ah, salvaged it," Jasmine admitted. "United Earth, actually."

"Huh," Duvall shrugged. "I always thought that the only way I'd see the inside of one of these was during a hostile boarding action."

"What do you think we're doing right now?" Jasmine asked. "Stay close."

Jasmine led the way deeper into the bowels of the ship, her eyes flitting constantly back and forth, as she watched for any sign of Kage – or any other hostile creature that might have found its way on board the ship. The floor beneath their feet was softer than she would have though possible for a military vessel. She knew that the spy ships in most navies were "softer" than typical military ships, but she had not really thought that the difference was all that great. Now she knew differently.

For starters, the research vessel was climate-controlled better than even the Fancy had been. In space, the confines of most space ships were hot and cramped. In space, most of the environmental problems were all about waste heat management. Computers, people and other equipment all generated heat and that heat had to go somewhere. When the vessel was exposed to the sun in the vacuum of space, there was nowhere for that heat to go. To make matters worse, the primary construction material of most human ships was metal. It was an excellent absorber and conductor of heat, but it didn't radiate heat out very well without air flowing around it to carry the heat off. Unlike normal planet-bound vehicles, one could not simply roll down the window to let out the excess heat. With nowhere to disperse the heat, the environmental systems of most ships were designed to keep the temperature at just below broiling hot. It was a miserable existence for merchant vessels, and a hellish one for military transports. Most Corps members had taken to walking around their berthing areas in nothing but their skivvies while not on duty. That, she recalled with no small sense of dark humor, had led to a strange occurrence of one hellishly bad sexually transmitted disease being shared by almost every single corporal and below in Charlie Company on board the Tres Chevaliers. She, fortunately, had been spared the indignity of that incident, having been a Staff Sergeant by then and privileged to be sharing a berthing space with two other NCOs.

This ship, as far as Jasmine could tell, had honest-to-God air conditioning.

The walls were actually decorated, something that Vincente had not bothered to share with her during his ill-fated attempt at inspecting the ship before. Small pictures of various liberty ports and planets – she recognized at least half of them from her time in the Corps – were hung throughout, creating a very homey atmosphere, one which she was not quite certain was proper United Earth military protocol. The floor was actually rubber-coated for comfort and ease on the knees, preventing the typical limp, which was usually something akin to a badge of honor among the other navies in the known universe.

"This ship," Jasmine sighed. "What a derp ship."

"Agreed," Duvall said.

"If this is roughing it, I should have gone into intelligence," Jasmine continued as she paused and motioned towards an open hatch. Duvall nodded in agreement and pressed herself up against the wall. Jasmine swiftly entered and crossed to the opposite corner, while Duvall followed quickly and broke to the right. Jasmine's eyes swept right and left, her gun following her eyes as she rapidly cleared the room.

"Clear," Jasmine announced. She let her guard down slightly as she inspected the room more closely. "This has to be the XO's room, maybe even the captain's cabin. This is some plush carpet."

"Next room?" Duvall asked.

"Yep," Jasmine said. "Mark the door and latch it."

As soon as they had exited the room, Duvall dogged the hatch and secured it from the outside. She then marked the door with a piece of wet IR chalk she produced from her pocket. Duvall then flipped on her IR light on her rifle, and satisfied with the reflective chalk's response to the IR, turned the light back off.

This process repeated for four more rooms before Jasmine began to grow irritated. She knew that Kage was on board somewhere, waiting for them. What she could not understand was its reluctance to attack the two women. Jasmine was more than willing to admit that both she and Duvall were extremely capable and dangerous women, but a Kaiju would not know that.

"This is getting old," Jasmine muttered. She banged the butt of her handgun on one of the walls. "Hey, bitch! I'm waiting for you! Come on out!"

Nothing. She grumbled under her breath and tried again. "C'mon, Kage. You're supposed to be some badass Kaiju. Prove me wrong, big boy. This is pathetic." She turned back to Duvall. "This motherfucker won't play with..." her voice trailed off.

Duvall's eyes were solid black pits, empty and unseeing. Her mouth was open in a silent scream, and her muscles appeared to be slack. She was no longer living. Jasmine could tell just by looking at her. Something controlled her, keeping her upright and standing.

Duvall's mouth twisted into a sickening, horrifying grin. Words tumbled out, oddly stilted and strangely accented.

"Human warrior... come out to play?"

"Oh, shit," Jasmine whispered. Her gun came up and she fired two shots into Duvall's forehead without conscious thought. Brain matter and blood splattered the wall and floor behind the marine captain. The grin grew slightly lopsided thanks to the damage caused by the massive .557 caliber rounds, but Duvall remained standing.

"Play time," dead Duvall said, and punched Jasmine in her chest armor. The plate cracked and Jasmine was thrown fifteen feet down the corridor. She would have gone further, had a wall not been there to thankfully slow her down. She felt the back plate crack as well when she hit the wall, but knew that the plates would eventually reform and solidify. The problem, she realized as she slowly picked herself up off the floor, was that she needed to stay alive long enough for that to happen.

Jasmine looked down and saw that she had somehow managed to hang onto her hand cannon. She brought it up and unloaded six more shots into the dead Duvall's body. The marine captain simply stood there and took the damage, not even flinching as the rounds struck her. Large chunks of flesh and blood flew from her body, but Kage – Jasmine was certain that the shadowy Kaiju had managed to possess the marine captain somehow – kept the body upright.

Jasmine tossed her handgun onto the floor and grabbed her kukri. She had anticipated that it could potentially turn into this sort of fight with the Kaiju. She hadn't counted on Duvall becoming a puppet of the Kaiju, however. Dead Duvall stuck a finger into one of the massive holes in her forehead and smiled at her.

Jasmine grimaced. "That's gross."

"Tickles," dead Duvall said with a shrug. More blood splashed onto the floor. "Human... bodies, weak, strange."

"Get out of hers then, and fight me with yours," Jasmine challenged.

"Play," dead Duvall said and moved.

Jasmine blinked as two sledgehammers slammed into her belly, knocking the air completely out of her. Another punch slammed into her face, rocking her head back and nearly breaking her neck. Two more rapid punches cracked another plate in her armor. She gasped as a familiar pain in her ribs flared. She'd broken enough of them to know the signs immediately when it happened.

Jasmine managed to duck another of dead Duvall's punches and stumble to her right, swinging her kukri wide and slicing one of dead Duvall's hamstrings. The marine captain did not even notice, pivoting on the very leg Jasmine had damaged. Dead Duvall punted Jasmine in the stomach, and Jasmine dropped to her hands and knees as tears formed in her eyes.

She rolled away and tried to get back on her feet. Her ribs, thoroughly bruised and battered at this point, made that difficult. She wheezed and struggled to breathe as she finally drew herself back up onto her feet. Her left hand clutched her ribs, while her right hung desperately onto the kukri.

"Bitch," Jasmine managed to gasp after a moment of effort.

"Play," dead Duvall said, her words echoing oddly in the hallway. "Human warrior..."

"Oh, fuck it," Jasmine said. She turned and began to limp down the hallway as fast as she could. She barely managed four steps before something violently yanked her back.

Something bone-numbingly cold pressed against her throat. She could smell the coppery tang of Duvall's blood in the breath of the animated corpse, and the steely strength in the dead woman's grip. A second hand twisted her left arm behind her back, and a cool breeze brushed against the back of her head.

"Fight me," dead Duvall hissed. "Fight the Darkness."

With her kukri still free, Jasmine flipped it over and stabbed Duvall in the mouth. Surprised, the corpse released her and Jasmine, not wasting a moment, jerked her kukri to the side, completely removing the upper half of Duvall's already-damaged head from her jaw. Dead Duvall twitched for a moment before the body fell to the ground, all semblance of life finally removed from the corpse. Jasmine wiped the bloody kukri on her pants leg and grimaced as more pain flared in her ribs. It was beginning to grow difficult to breathe and purple spots were starting to form in her eyes.

"Stupid Kaiju," she whispered painfully and began to walk away. Something caught her eye, though. She stopped and looked back at Duvall. A shadow emerged from the body, slowly rising to its feet. The pitch black shadow absorbed all of the light in the hall, almost as if a black hole had opened up right there in the middle of the ship. The shadow became a solid form and Jasmine felt the air grow colder in the already chilly ship.

Kage, in all his full and majestic glory, stood before her.

He was very man-shaped, she decided as she gave him the once over, though he appeared to have eight arms instead of two. Four eyes, bright azure and burning with intensity, stared through her. The body of the Kaiju seemed to both expand and contract simultaneously as she stared at it, the effect giving her stomach some mild distress.

"So... this is the mighty Kage," Jasmine said as adrenaline began to flow into her system, blocking out the pain temporarily and giving her a bit of wind. She wiped away a small trickle of blood, which had begun to run down from her scalp. She spat onto the floor.

The shadow bowed majestically, mockingly. The eyes of the Kaiju seemed to twinkle merrily now, the blue still bright and clear, the shadow still black and empty. It seemed to be content to let things be, as though it knew what she needed – and what she had to do. Jasmine scowled, but she continued to force herself to wait to make the Kaiju move first. It would be her only shot at survival.

Kage moved forward, the shadow swaying from side to side as it approached, the tendrils of each arm dipping from the low ceiling to the floor. The Kaiju seemed to fill the entire corridor as it drew closer. Jasmine swallowed and double-checked the grip of her kukri. A thin coat of blood – both hers and Duvall's – intermingled with her sweat, which made her slightly nervous. The kukri seemed to be a far more effective weapon against the Kaiju than her gun had been, and she did not want to lose the large blade.

A tentacle shadow shot out suddenly, the arm evolving into a point as it thrust forward. Jasmine nimbly jumped to the side and slashed the tip off, causing the Kaiju to retract the shadowy arm quickly. The darkness shrunk slightly as Kage paused, reassessing the human woman. Jasmine smirked and realized that the Kaiju had never fought anything like her before. She took a step forward, and the Kaiju backed away the tiniest bit.

Emboldened, she took another. Still Kage backed away. A tiny smidgen of confidence returned to her soul.

"Oh, didn't like that, did we?" Jasmine smiled and waved the kukri in the air. A thin beam of light reflecting off one of the hall lights swept across the Kaiju. It recoiled slightly. A thought suddenly struck her like thunder. "You're a one-trick pony, aren't you? That's why you don't run this place."

Kage attacked again, this time two of the shadowy arms launching themselves at her. Jasmine managed to dodge one, but the second struck her solidly in the thigh, the shadowy point driving through her pants armor with relative ease. She howled as the arm quickly retracted, her left leg suddenly weak. She shifted her weight as Kage, sensing weakness in his opponent, charged forward.

Good quality steel blocked each shadowy attack as Jasmine fought for her life against the Kaiju. Her blade flashed through the darkness, hacking, slashing, stabbing, doing everything she could to defeat the Kaiju, to win. Even as she fought, though, she was keenly aware of her strength ebbing slowly away as she continued to bleed from the nasty wound in her leg. Her lungs began to burn as her broken ribs protested her rough treatment of them, and her head began to swim from the lack of oxygen.

She would not quit, would not give up. She was Defense Corps, and they did not acknowledge the existence of the word quit.

Another strike from the Kaiju broke through her defenses, slashing her open from hip to thigh. She cried out and wildly swung her kukri, which connected with Kage's chest. The Kaiju staggered back at the same time she stumbled forward, her wounds too great for her to stand steadily any longer. She thrust again with the kukri, which, while not typically a stabbing blade, still featured enough of a tip. This sharp point drove itself into where Jasmine had guessed Kage's throat was. She was rewarded with a noticeable drop in the size of the Kaiju as the shadow contracted in on itself, clearly wounded. She fell to her knees, and with her last ounce of strength, separated Kage's feet from the rest of his body.

A thin, high-pitched scream erupted from the center of the Kaiju's mass. The shadow flopped down onto the floor, tentacle-arms twitching uncontrollably. One shot out and pierced through her left collarbone, cleanly snapping the clavicle and narrowly missing the internal carotid artery. She howled in pain and began to hack furiously at the Kaiju with her kukri, dismembering the creature even as the loss of blood and energy claimed her.

****

Vincente was resting his back against the Aardvark, his vision slightly blurred still from the painkillers that Jasmine had pumped into him before she and Captain Duvall disappeared into the military ship. That had been three hours before, and while he was still in some pain, it had yet to return in full force.

Unfortunately, Jasmine and Duvall hadn't returned either.

Next to him, a marine corpsman knelt down and checked him over again. A butterfly bandage had pulled his cheek back together, and the medic seemed pleased with the lack of new blood. His puncture wounds, while bloody, had actually not done any vital damage. Assuming that he could get on the ship and make his way off-planet, he might actually survive.

Of course, that did nothing for his other problem: how to lie to Hines about what he had found.

"You are good to go, Captain," the marine said respectfully.

"Help me up then," Vincente grunted. The corpsman assisted him to his feet. He swayed slightly but managed to stay upright, partially due to the marine's strong arms. He waved off the marine. "I'm good, I'm okay. I want to go check on my merc."

"He needs a true medical facility," the corpsman told him. "Please get him to one such facility within forty hours and he will probably live. Any longer and you begin to run the risk of sepsis settling in. Then you are looking at kidney failure, organ failure, et cetera. Do you understand me, sir?"

"Trust me, we're getting to a qualified trauma center as soon as possible," Vincente confirmed. "Preferably one in Zubulun space, as far away from United Earth as we can get."

"I am sure that such accommodations can be arranged," the corpsman nodded. Marines suddenly sprang into action around them, running towards Vincente's new ship. Vincente looked around and saw that a few others had struggled to get the severely wounded Yolo onto his feet and away from the vessel.

As rifles were trained onto the open airlock of the vessel, Vincente tried to get a good look of whatever was coming out. Marines stood nervously by, hoping that it was the two women but dreading that it was a Kaiju. Vincente found his hand itching towards his empty holster and chided himself. There was little he could do, in any case. He was banged up worse than any other time in his life.

A familiar blonde head came out of the airlock and Vincente felt a smile threaten to split his face wide open. Jasmine, pale and covered in blood and gore, stumbled out of the airlock. She was trailing blood from quite a few puncture wounds, including one he saw in her upper thigh, which should have prevented her from walking at all. In her hand, she clung to something large and dark.

She blinked as she looked around, uncertainty on her face as she sought out something. She tossed the head of Kage into the sand and limped over to where Yolo was. She knelt down next to the man, took his head in both of her hands, and kissed him fiercely.

Vincente's eyes nearly bugged out of his head as Jasmine continued to kiss the mercenary. Yolo, who had been initially too shocked to kiss back, was now returning it with passion and authority. A few of the marines looked away, slightly embarrassed at the scene, while still others cheered the two on or teased them about it.

Vincente cleared his throat loudly. Jasmine gave him the bird and continued to kiss the mercenary. Vincente shook his head and chuckled.

"Let the boy breathe," he told her. "He's pretty banged up."

Reluctantly, Jasmine released Yolo's head. She looked around at the marines before finally meeting Vincente's eye.

"Duvall didn't make it," she said.

"I'm sorry," Vincente said, and was surprised to find that he truly meant it.

"Boss?"

"Yeah?"

"No offenses intended to our wonderful Zubulun friends, but let's get off this fucking planet as soon as possible."

Vincente nodded and laughed. "Yes. Let's."

INTERLUDE VI

"Somebody had better start answering my questions," the Prosecutor said as the last Wild One had been taken from the interrogation room. He sighed and looked at the four guards who remained. None of them had so much as said a word since he had arrived six hours before and began to interrogate all persons of interest in what had begun to be called the Huerta Event by everyone involved.

No matter. He had everything he was looking for, save one vital piece of the puzzle: the location of Vincente Huerta himself.

His head suddenly snapped around as the door swung wide open. A man, dressed similarly to him, bustled into the room. He stopped as he looked at the man seated in what was supposed to be his chair. He tilted his head and frowned.

"Excuse me, but I'm Special Prosecutor William Cloyd," the new arrival announced as he gave the man in the chair a piercing look. "Who are you?"

"Nobody in particular," the man said as he pushed his chair out and stood. The four guards suddenly looked around, surprised. "Thank you for the use of your facilities." He began to walk out the door.

"Stop him," Cloyd ordered the guards. The man sighed as the two closest prevented him from leaving. The man turned and looked at the new arrival. "Who are you?" Cloyd demanded.

"I don't answer to you," the man retorted. "That's all you need to know."

"Not quite," the special prosecutor smiled narrowly. He made a motion to his guards, a gesture which managed to convey both a promise and a threat simultaneously. He was a professional, after all. "I can... entice you to answers my questions."

"My name is... Hines."

"And what are you doing here, Mister Hines?"

"Using your facilities to conduct a Code Yellow inquiry."

"I see." The special prosecutor did not see, but William Cloyd had not risen to his position by being stupid. He knew what a Code

Yellow was, even if the guards in the room did not. He nodded. "I'm sorry to bother you, sir. Guards, let him go."

Hines walked out of the room, silently fuming. Using the Code Yellow meant that nobody would interfere with him any longer and he would have carte blanche to roam the narrow confines of the space station unimpeded. It also meant that his cover was now blown, since lowly guards could never be trusted to keep their mouths shut. Within hours, everyone there would know that one Vincente Huerta had bamboozled the most powerful military in this region of space. Details would spread. The story of Captain Huerta would grow with each retelling, and it would soon be legend.

That, Hines thought as he disappeared down a shadowy, abandoned hallway of the massive station, was the one thing I was trying to prevent. Looks like this is the end of my investigation. Time to start the cover up. Damn it. Too many loose ends. Oh well. The general consensus is that Huerta and his crew died on that world. I guess our secret is still safe. For now, at least. Just one thing bothers me...

Captain... if you're still alive... where in the Hell are you hiding? Why can't I find you?

EPILOGUE

The beach was blindingly white, but the man didn't care. Once out of shape, pasty white and greying, he was now a perfect picture of a wealthy retiree: toned, tanned, with raven-black hair. Scars ran up and down his body, leading quite a few of the attractive women who noticed him to wonder and whisper about the man.

Some thought he was a retired pirate. Others, a former Special Forces operative who was medically discharged. None of them could ever guess the truth, however. The truth was far stranger than any fiction that they could come up with.

To his left lay a stunningly beautiful woman lounging in a beach chair. She wore a floppy hat to protect her face from the harsh glare of the planet's sun, but countered this with the skimpiest two-piece bikini she could legally get away with. Her body was unblemished by scars, courtesy of skilled plastic surgeons and a lot of money. Her clear blue eyes were hidden behind a pair of protective glasses.

On her other side was the largest, most muscular man anyone had ever seen. He, much like his compatriot, had dozens of nasty scars crossing his body, including a long one, which ran from the center of his chest until it disappeared under his bathing shorts. He looked as if he could literally pick a man up and break him with his bare hands. He seemed a quiet man, however, not prone to much discussion about his deeds, his past, or his scars. Many women on the beach wondered just how far down that particular scar went, and if his obvious paramour would mind if they investigated.

Mostly, however, the group was admired from a distance. They carried Zubulun passports, which made them exotic enough. The fact that they owned half of the beach everyone was currently enjoying instilled just enough fear in people to leave them alone. After all, they reasonably thought, who wanted to cross reputed Zubulun crime lords?

"Gotta admit, I didn't think that they'd keep up their end of the bargain," Vincente said as he reached out and grabbed the beer from the holder on his seat. He took a swig from the cold bottle and smacked his lips appreciatively. "Ah, good stuff."

"I didn't doubt Dandridge," Jasmine said as she gently squeezed Yolo's much larger hand. "It was the rest of them who I doubted."

"This place is nice," Yolo murmured sleepily.

Silence stretched out between the trios as each lost themselves. Vincente tilted his beer towards the crashing waves before them. "For those who didn't come back."

"Amen." Jasmine whispered.

"Poor Hector," Yolo said, his voice filled with sadness. "He was a good boss. It just wasn't fair."

Vincente took a sip from his beer and looked out at the horizon. He sighed and glanced to his right, where an attractive woman lay alarmingly close to him. He gave the woman a smile before looking away. He shifted his gaze back to Jasmine and growled under his breath.

"I still don't see why you had to tell my wife we were here, though."

"She loves you, Vincente. Especially since you lost like thirty pounds. You actually resemble attractive again. That does a lot to rekindle the flame, you know."

He sighed. "She just loves my money."

"If it was just that, she would have left when you paid her the money you owed," Jasmine needlessly reminded him. "Besides, you know she can hear you, right?"

"I know she can hear me," Vincente aid. "Two reasons I don't care: one, like you said, she's still here. Two, she can't have a gun on her to shoot me with. Not with that tiny bathing suit."

A laugh filled the air, gentle and loving. "Darling, you still don't understand foreplay. If you did, you would have found it three days ago."

Vincente was silent for a moment before he finally said anything. When he finally did, it was a well tolerated, "Frag it."

They laughed. They drank. They cried. They drank some more. Vincente quietly kissed his wife. Jasmine kissed her paramour noisily. They were happy. They grew sad. Then happy again. They all drank some more.

The group remained on the beach until long after dark, drinking to remember, drinking to forget.

THE END

www.ingramcontent.com/pod-product-compliance
Lightning Source LLC
Chambersburg PA
CBHW061240170626
46809CB00007B/2757